Richard Meade Bache

Vulgarisms and Other Errors of Speech

Including a chapter on taste, and one containing examples of bad taste

Richard Meade Bache

Vulgarisms and Other Errors of Speech
Including a chapter on taste, and one containing examples of bad taste

ISBN/EAN: 9783337410230

Printed in Europe, USA, Canada, Australia, Japan

Cover: Foto ©Andreas Hilbeck / pixelio.de

More available books at **www.hansebooks.com**

VULGARISMS

AND

OTHER ERRORS OF SPEECH:

INCLUDING

A CHAPTER ON TASTE,

AND ONE

CONTAINING EXAMPLES OF BAD TASTE.

PHILADELPHIA:

CLAXTON, REMSEN & HAFFELFINGER,

819 and 821 MARKET STREET.

———

1868.

PREFACE.

Many persons, although they have not enjoyed advantages early in life, have, through merit combined with the unrivalled opportunities which this country presents, risen to station in society. Few of them, it must be thought, even if unaware of the extent of their deficiency in knowledge of their language, are so obtuse as not to perceive their deficiency at all, and not to know that it often presents them in an unfavourable light in their association with the more favoured children of fortune. Few, it must be believed, would not from one motive or the other, from desire for knowledge, or from dread of ridicule, gladly avail themselves of opportunities for instruction. And no one who has travelled, and has seen everywhere, in cars, steamboats, hotels, streets, crowds of well-dressed, presentable people murdering the King's English, will say that, with all that our Public Schools accomplish, there is not much room for improvement, and that much instruction is not still needed.

In view of this, the author conceived that a small work, treating of the most prevalent and gross errors in English, would be an acceptable addition to our

books on education; especially, if incorporated in it
were some information regarding certain improprie-
ties of speech, which in one sense are not errors, but
which, in another, are errors, and at once fix the
speaker's grade as low in refinement. He also
thought that the work might prove suggestive to
other writers to occupy the same field.

It is folly to suppose that the progress of error in
language cannot be stayed, and that we must give
way to every innovation. Language, created by man
in the exercise of the divine gift of the faculty of
speech, is still a slave to execute his bidding. He
can fashion it to serve his purpose in any direction
that he sees fit; and because, generally, he does not
do so deliberately, with express purpose to accomplish
each end in view, but does so mechanically, he is not
less the absolute master of its destiny. It is a truism
to say that, without innovation, there can be no progress in language. It is not progress that any one
should wish to impede. It is not innovation, therefore, that is reprehensible, but innovation without
good cause, and, worst of all, innovation for innovation's sake. There are, in language, progressive
forces in the mass of the people; conservative forces,
in the body of the highly educated. The due pro-
portional action of each is necessary to its salutary
development and conservation.

With few exceptions, the errors herein noticed are not only errors, but vulgarisms; for, be it known, an error of speech is not necessarily a vulgarism, nor is a vulgarism necessarily an error of speech, although a vulgarism does generally combine with the fault of exclusive use by the uneducated, that of being intrinsically wrong. From an occasional lapse, no one, however well educated, is exempt; but such a mistake cannot properly be termed a vulgarism, unless it is one that is habitually made by the illiterate: it is an isolated blunder, associated with nothing but human fallibility. If, on the contrary, a word or a phrase, absolutely correct in itself, comes into use so current as to be associated with the illiterate only, it falls from its high estate and becomes a vulgarism; and its degradation cannot be in any degree redeemed, either by its intrinsic accuracy, or by the education of the utterer. A few years ago, no one of education would have scrupled to assent to an expression of opinion, by replying, "That is so;" but the use of the phrase, since that time, as a byword, has reduced it to the level of the lowest vulgarism, and driven it out of correct usage.

Throughout this work constantly occur the terms "vulgarism," "the vulgar," "vulgarity." The connection in which they are used together, and the similarity of the words, coming as they do from a common stock, may lead some readers to think that the author believes them to be correlative terms. This is not the case. The phrase "the vulgar" has two distinct meanings. In one, it signifies merely the illiterate; in the other, it signifies the pretentious: those who, to whatever station they may claim to belong, are in a false position. One may be illiterate and not be vulgar; one may be literate and even highly gifted, and yet be vulgar; and lastly, one may be both illiterate *and* vulgar. One out of his sphere, occupying a position for which he is not fitted by nature or by education, or by both, is vulgar, whether he was born in a hovel or in a palace. Vulgarity depends entirely on the relative refinement of the sphere in which one moves. Complete immunity from it is the privilege of no society. Therefore, to one sense of the phrase " the vulgar," must the idea of "vulgarity" be attached. To the other sense, meaning merely the illiterate, belongs the word "vulgarisms," which may more properly be termed illiteracies.

The reason why those very errors which are not held to be disgraceful as belonging to one class of people are rightly imputed as disgraceful to another class, is solely because the sense of justice in all society holds none accountable for ignorance of what they never had an opportunity to learn, while it visits with ridicule those who, surrounded by all the usual accompaniments of high station and by facilities for acquiring education, seem not to notice that in the brilliant setting of their life is absent the jewel which only can confer lustre on rank. The world sees the sham, laughs at it, and probably will laugh at it to the end of time.

If, before reading these lines, persons of more general information than those for whom this work is designed, should have chanced to read the introductory chapter on 'The Study of English,' they may have been surprised that the author should not have qualified his praise of English erudition by mentioning the fact that a late Report to Parliament proves that, in the English Public Schools, Colleges, and Universities, there is no special training in the language of the country. * The author, deeming that the fact does not militate against the assertion which he made in that chapter, purposely omitted mention of it there, in order to avoid a long digression, and reserved his notice of it for this as the more appropriate place.

---

* The 'Report of Her Majesty's Commissioners appointed to inquire into the management of certain Colleges and Schools,' presented to Parliament, March, 1864.

In the chapter on 'The Study of English' there is to be found no assertion that in English institutions of learning sufficient attention is paid to the study of the vernacular. Not entertaining that belief, the author could not have made that assertion. Long before the Report to Parliament made public the state of affairs, he was sure of the fact which the Report establishes. It had from time to time been deplored by English writers. English schools, then, are admitted and always have been admitted by him to be lamentably deficient in affording special training in the native language. What he asserted was, that the thoroughness of English education (thorough except in the one particular under consideration), created a large body of conservatives in language, and this he reaffirms.

Many believe that school is a great treasury of knowledge, whence each scholar bears away all the wealth of knowledge which he will ever be capable of transporting. Much more properly may it be likened to a mental gymnasium, whence the faculties, improved by daily exercise, go forth into the world and grapple with realities tasking all their powers and, after accomplishing wonders, still leave undescried possibilities for the efforts of future minds. Why is it that the study of the Greek language, for which few of those who learn it find use after quitting the academic halls, has always been held in high estimation? Simply because the perfection of its construction, and its philosophic genius, render the study of it an admirable mental discipline.

While one may admit, as the English themselves do, that their scholastic courses neglect the study of the native language, one may at the same time maintain that the scholars themselves are a force conservative of the language Leaving School, College, or University, the English youth leave them with no superficial instruction. In whatever they have learned, they are well grounded. The thoroughness of their training in the classical languages has been some training in their own language; the station which, as a mass, they occupy in society, is a still more efficient means of training in it; and many of them, after leaving the institutions in which they were educated, pay special attention to it, their knowledge of other languages being a basis for sure and rapid progress. In any case, being highly educated, they form necessarily a highly conservative body of men, and the literary power vested in them is more efficient from being centralized in large universities and cities, to which they, as educated men, naturally gravitate, and to which the country looks with deference as authority in language. That, in this condition of affairs, as compared with ours, corruption has less chance successfully to attack and injure the purity of the language, will probably be generally conceded.

The author trusts that he does not flatter himself in thinking that his work is all that it professes to be. Whether it can effect any good, only the Public can decide, and to them he commits it in the hope of its meeting with their approbation.

CONTENTS.

CHAPTER I.

THE STUDY OF ENGLISH.

THE study of English by those whose native language it is, has increased in favour since, of late, in England and in the United States, the question has been discussed, Whether, even conceding that too much attention is not paid to Greek and Latin, too little is not paid to the modern languages, and especially to English.

In England, when education was possessed by few, those, of course, belonged to the aristocracy, to the gentry, and to the "middle classes," whose homes and society were schools of the native language. Under the circumstances, it is natural that the classical languages should have unduly enlisted the attention of teachers, as necessary to be imparted to youth; not only on account of their intrinsic beauty, and that of the works composed in them, but on account of the insight which they give into English itself.*

* "There be two special considerations which keep the Latin and other learned tongues, though chiefly the Latin,

Such education, inapplicable in the course of time to England,—for, with increased knowledge among all classes, she has outgrown the ideas upon which it was based,—was always inapplicable to this country, where stability of government depends, not on mere Democracy, but on an *educated* democracy;—the capacity of an educated *people* to administer a Government "of the people, by the people, and for

in great countenance among us: the one is the knowledge which is registered in them; the other is the conference which the learned of Europe do commonly use by them, both in speaking and writing. We seek them for profit, and keep them for that conference; but whatever else may be done in our tongue, either to serve private use or the beautifying our speech, I do not see but it may well be admitted, *even though in the end it displaced the Latin,* as the Latin did others, and furnished itself by the Latin learning. For is it not indeed a marvellous bondage to become servants to one tongue, for learning' sake, the most of our time, with loss of most time, whereas we may have the very same treasure in our own tongue, with the gain of most time?—our own bearing the joyful title of our liberty and freedom, the Latin tongue remembering us of our thraldom. I honour the Latin; but I worship the English."—Mulcaster, Master of St. Paul's School, as quoted by Isaac Disraeli, in his 'Amenities of Literature.'

the people;"—where education must be general in its diffusion, and practical in its character.

Nevertheless, education in this country, except that in the Public Schools, partook of the English practice of cultivating the classical languages, and comparatively neglecting the vernacular; until within a very few years, when commenced a powerful and still progressive movement, in favour of introducing many practical branches of study. This movement has already effected great changes in the former scholastic courses, and one evidence of its power is to be found in the interest awakened to the study of English. Even within a few months, this interest has been manifested anew, by the publication of several works which have attracted attention both in England and in this country, and given increased impulse to the study.

The first of these works, consisting of a series of articles contributed by the Rev. Henry Alford, Dean of Canterbury, to an English periodical called 'Good Words,' and afterwards revised and published in a volume entitled 'The Queen's English,' brought out a host of critics

in England and Scotland. An interesting literary tournament ensued, in which the lists were
relinquished to Dean Alford, and a Mr. G.
Washington Moon, now well-known, by whom
the Dean, after a spirited contest, was signally
worsted. Yet, although Mr. Moon convicts the
Dean of many flagrant errors, the work of the
latter contains much valuable information. It
is, however, a dangerous work to peruse, unless
the reader possesses some critical knowledge.

Dean Alford's book had also the effect of in-
citing Mr. Edward S. Gould to publish his work
entitled 'Good English.' Mr. Moon's new-gained
celebrity led to his writing critical essays for the
'Round Table;' in the course of which essays,
he criticised the style of the Hon. George P.
Marsh's contributions to the 'Nation.'*

That these writings have had, and will con-
tinue to have, a beneficial effect, in instructing,
and in leading to still farther study of our language, is very evident. But although, consider-

---

* At the present writing, there is progressing, in the
'Round Table,' a controversy between Mr. Moon and Mr.
Gould, in relation to the general accuracy of Mr. Gould's
book.

ing their character, they enjoy a wide circulation, it is relatively circumscribed, as is also the case with the standard works by Kames, Campbell, Blair, Trench, Harrison, Lowth, Priestley, Walker, Sheridan, and others. Their influence on the people, to whatever degree existing, is indirect. In general, the points discussed consist of niceties in language, far above the popular range. Most philologists suffer to pass unnoticed, as if unworthy of their attention, errors which they know must eventually establish themselves in the language; for none know so well as they, that language is made chiefly by the people,* and that whatever error in it the people definitively stamp with their approval, ceases to be spurious, and becomes genuine coinage.

Our language has heretofore sensibly improved, and it is now remarkable for its energy, copiousness, and elegance. It is important that, while we admit it may still farther advance, we should put in action forces conservative of its

* The great philosopher, the great man of science, the poet, and others, often coin words by the prescriptive right of genius.

purity, and determine that, while it shall not be restricted in aught that will add to its power, it shall be kept from degradation.

To this point, Mr. Moon, in his Preface to the fourth edition of his book, approvingly quotes Schlegel, who says: "The care of the national language is at all times a sacred trust. Every man of education should make it the object of his unceasing concern to preserve his language pure." Dean Alford remarks, that "the language of a people is no trifle. The national mind is reflected in the national speech."

It especially behooves us, who possess no Academy, like that of the French, no cities in which literary power is concentrated, to know, and to act upon the knowledge, that we lack the conservative elements which maintain the integrity of a language. Granting the continued existence of Paris and the French Academy, and that of London and the English Universities, the people in the rest of the respective countries containing those centres of learning might speak what jargon they please, the French language, and the English language, would be preserved in their purity, although, necessarily, they would cease to be progressive.* From such centres go forth the laws—not affirmed by decrees, but by usage—that regulate and control the language of a country. They, in the

* Dean Trench says: "The French Academy, containing the great body of the distinguished literary men of France, once sought to exercise such a domination over their own language, and if any could have succeeded, might have hoped to do so. But the language recked of their decrees as little as the advancing ocean did of those of Canute. They were obliged to give way, and in each successive edition of their Dictionary to throw open its doors to words which had established themselves in the language, and would hold their ground, comparatively indifferent whether they received the Academy's seal of allowance or no."

The Academy, no doubt, expected and attempted too much; but that it exercises great influence on the language should be apparent. Is it to be supposed that works so admirable as the tomes which the Academy elaborates· with the greatest care have no influence on French writers! Through them, the influence of the Academy is felt. The Academy exercises just such a conservative influence as does any body of the educated —with this advantage, that it has the weight derived from the literary distinction of its members, from organization, and from publication. That it sways great power is susceptible of demonstration, but the fact stands to reason.

cases instanced, may not be able to teach the
the cockney elegant English, nor the *badaud**
elegant French; but, at least, the languages are
safe from the illiterate of both capital and pro-
vince.   The provincial language of England and
of France has never, as is the case in our country, been the same as that of the great towns
and cities; but if pure language has not permeated
the provinces, it has, to make amends, been preserved in its own purity.

In this country, the same language is spoken
from the Atlantic to the Pacific, from the Lakes
to the Gulf of Mexico. What regulates it?
The best usage of the mother country is not
generally regarded as binding, and no city, no
district of our own, can lay down law which will
be obeyed.   We are, at the same time, a people
inhabiting a country vast in extent, varied in
climate, amid new scenes, and surrounded by un-
precedented elements of progress: circumstances, each of which is capable of causing great
accessions to and alterations in language.   All
the causes which, unheeded, tend to degrade a

* The Parisian cockney.

language, are in full action among us, and scarcely any of the conservative ones to keep them in check. We read and write prodigiously. We are great talkers of slang and contemners of usage. We have no court of appeal.*

This country is certainly destined to be inhabited by a greater number of English-speaking people than will occupy any other portion of the globe; judge then of the influence, for good or

---

* When the writer remarks that there is, in this country, no recognized authority in English, he refers merely to the non-recognition of a superior usage emanating from some city, district, or country. He does not mean to assert that there is among us no recognition of fixed grammatical principles, which, saving some few trifling points unsettled, regulate the mutual dependence and arrangement of words and clauses, however much the rules deduced from them may be infringed, and still leave the language comprehensible. To be explicit then:—Americans recognize, in pronunciation, no supreme authority or *standard;* but, in the construction of their language, they recognize a standard of fixed grammatical principles and rules. In England, France, and the other countries of Europe, both are recognized. The reason for the difference is that there is not, in this country, as there is in Europe, a distinct body of people of education and refinement, whose words make the law in words

for evil, that it must exercise on our mother-tongue. Would it not be well if we, until there shall exist among us some recognized authority, some supreme arbiter in language, should individually exercise greater care in it, and also invite discussion of it among ourselves, thereby exposing flagrant popular errors of the day, which otherwise will soon become engrafted on it.

There is, in this country, attending the reaction in ideas about education, danger of temporary error, from which England is exempt, owing to the conservative power mentioned, derived from the amount, character, and centralization of education in that country. *

* If we consider the youth of this country, as compared with the age of England, we shall be able, without humiliation, to acknowledge that, in the aggregate, the education here is inferior. But whether we can or cannot perceive it, will or will not acknowledge it, it is a fact. To use a homely illustration:—If education in the respective countries could be boiled down in separate pots, England's, or, more properly, Great Britain's would afford the larger yield. Her books, her newspapers, her magazines, show by their number, and by their character, that they cater for an aggregate of cultivated taste greater than that in

The reaction unhappily chimes in with an idea too popular here, depreciatory of the higher orders of education. Owing to the circumstance that the people have not realized the object to be attained by a finished education, because the education which generally they possess, answers their present needs, an undervaluation of it for its own sake, of all knowledge that is not considered *practical*,—by which expression is meant, *not directly convertible into money*,—has become quite prevalent.

This is an extreme to be as carefully avoided as the one which devotes to the study of the classics the greater portion of the time at the disposal of most of our youth, thereby neglecting the so-called practical, and *really* valuable, studies which are happily coming more and more into vogue.

this country. Her ancient civilization, the structure of her society, her great seats of learning, the incentives which she holds forth to literary distinction, fully account for this fact. We have many people educated; she has fewer, but better educated. Her education being centralized in her Universities, and in her large towns and cities, exerts a commanding influence over the language and literature of the whole country.

Edward Everett said, in some remarks which he made before the Cambridge High School: "I hold, sir, that to read the English language well, that is, with intelligence, feeling, spirit, and effect; to write, with despatch, a neat, handsome, legible hand, (for it is, after all, a great object in writing to have others able to read what you write;) and to be master of the four rules of arithmetic, so as to dispose at once with accuracy of every question of figures which comes up in practical life,—I say I call this a good education; and if you add the ability to write pure grammatical English, with the help of very few hard words, I regard it as an excellent education."*

How many reach this standard? Even if many do, what might have been true, would, with a higher grade of general education, cease to be true. He who thus defined education, when it reached a certain point, to be good, and when it reached a certain other point, to be excellent, would have been one of the last men to argue that a higher education is not desirable, and that the opportunity to acquire it is not to be eagerly seized.

* Everett's Works, Vol. II., pp. 601, 602.

It is a great error to hold that all education beyond reading, writing, and arithmetic, is a waste of time. This observation may at first sight appear to the reader to offer a gratuitous insult to the good sense of the people; but it is nevertheless true, that thousands of persons who should know better entertain that opinion; and this is the case among many of those constituting what is called the business-community, a very large class in this country.

All knowledge is practical. It is a chain consisting of an infinite number of links, of which we cannot precisely determine the relative value. Ignorance of this, conspiring with the reaction that has set in against "non-practical education," can hardly fail to prove gravely prejudicial to the cause of enlightenment in our country.

CHAPTER II.

SLANG.

BEFORE treating of errors in speech, the way for the subject should be prepared, by exposing certain practices which, although not errors in the sense in which the word was previously used, are hurtful to language.

First in order among these shall be noticed—as it is first in importance—the language called *slang*, which pervades too much of the conversation even of the refined. Harrison remarks, that " Colonization has a tendency not only to add to the words of a language, but also to corrupt it. New scenes, new objects, new habits of life, call forth new expressions, at the same time that words, in many cases, deviate from their original signification. Many words have crept into the English language, in America, which are quite new to it; others have changed their meaning; others are merely fanciful. From America, we have adopted to *progress*, to *effectuate*. *Clever*, in America, has gained a meaning which it does not express in England; as, a *clever house*, a *clever son*, a *clever cargo*. *Slick, kedge, boss, absquatulate*, are from America; nor do we quite understand what is meant by a *tall* smell."

It would be easy to cite many examples in which words have either deviated unwarrantably from their primitive meanings, or, retaining those meanings, have subserved the purpose of slang.

It is not desirable that people should ceaselessly strive to speak with elegance every sentence which they utter; if they did, all conversation would be stilted: but it certainly is desirable that slang should not be recognized as an acceptable addition to the language of the educated. In the writer's hearing, not long since, a very respectable man, who has some pretension to education, inasmuch as he is a publisher, found no better expression to describe the position of an influential person in a certain business, than to say, that he was "at the top of the heap." Slang is especially offensive in woman, to whom we are pleased to ascribe delicacy of taste. Yet how often do we not hear her introduce it into conversation! "He has the stamps," said, lately, in a public place, a young woman who would have been mortified to think that she had produced a bad impression even on a bystander.

On occasions, very rarely, a slang expression may with propriety be used, to describe what is otherwise indescribable. Nothing but *hifalutin* can at present convey to us the idea of the most vapid sort of bombast; nothing but *spread-eagle*, that of the style of the Fourth-of-July oration of the past; nothing but *shoddy*, the grandeur of vulgar insignificance. But let even these, and similar words, die with the occasions that gave them birth. They may be tolerated in the conversation of friends. If they may be suffered to pass there, which is questionable, they are inadmissible in addressing a stranger, or a slight acquaintance. Familiarity is insulting, and slang is familiar. Let it never be considered as having a foothold in our language, but as separate and apart as is the cant of thieves and gypsies. "You git," and "I bet," may, in the frontier-like life of California, serve well enough to express "Get out," and "You may rest assured that I will;" but a higher general civilization scorns such phrases.*

Enough has been said on this topic. The memory of every one will suggest many examples in point.

* It must not be inferred from this remark, that civilization in California is of a low grade. A new country is necessarily settled by adventurers of an inferior as well as of a superior class. The former, in such a region, acquire a prominence which they can no longer maintain when it is well populated. Probably no city in the world, of equal size, can exhibit a population superior to that of San Francisco.

CHAPTER III.

WANT OF SIMPLICITY.

NEXT in faultiness to the use of slang, comes the practice of using exaggerated expressions, in speaking or in writing about the simplest subjects.

In this, a certain allowance must be made in the case of youth, and in that of the language of compliment, by whomsoever used, young or old. Youth is so imaginative, that its enthusiasm irradiates whatever comes within its view; so inexperienced, that it does not comprehend the relations of things. Compliment is so well-established as the language of insincerity, that, to convey sincere praise,—to avoid the appearance of flattery,—it must be conveyed indirectly, by implication, or else with the frank assertion that what is said is not intended as a *mere compliment*. This is only another way of saying that compliment is the language of exaggeration, for truth is clothed only in the language of simplicity. Nevertheless, by one of those subtle processes by

which the mind seeks to deceive itself, it is osten-
sibly given and received as something, while,
really, it is regarded as nothing.

With all due admission of the qualifications
noted, the use of inapplicable terms and exaggerated expressions is far too common. "It
was an *awfully* hot day." "I suffered in the
cars, *frightfully*, from heat." "When we reached
our destination, we had a *horrible* dinner." Why
not go a step farther, and say, "I was obliged to
occupy an *appalling* bed for the night?"

This extravagant style does not always proceed from inexperience of life; it is very frequently cultivated, under the impression that it
enhances the interest of what is said. But what
is the real effect? All beauty in nature, all
beauty in art, consist in proportion, in delicacy
of light and shade and colour, judicious contrast,
blending into one harmonious effect. In this
style, the matter is obscured by incongruous
materials. Besides, the word-painter has used
them so lavishly, that they will not last him,
however abundant they may be. In such a
style, the words do not represent the ideas which
the speaker should wish to convey. They have

no fixed value. They must be judged by the
criterion of each individual's character and education; whereas, they should have a standard
value.

The most flagrant instance of this vicious
mode of expression, that ever came under the
notice of the writer, was heard by him a few
months ago, in a street-car. As the car rolled
along, a young woman, bedizened with finery,
and fluent in speech, descanted, partly for the
benefit of her companion, and partly for that of
the rest of the passengers, on the stores and
other places of business on the route. Everything attracted her attention, excited her enthusiasm, and prompted her remarks. Her volu-
bility was quite unequal to the task of keeping
pace with the quick succession of her frivolous
ideas.

The first store to which she directed the attention of her companion, she called *elegant*.
That was not very wrong, although the store
was not elegant; but, having employed a super-
lative term to describe a thing of moderate pre-
tensions, the next store, more attractive to her,
received the compound epithet, *splendid-elegant*.

Curious to know what expression could be in reserve, the writer listened attentively. The car soon passed a combined restaurant and confectionery. Doubtless, the pleasant recollection of some lunch after shopping, or supper after the theatre, flashed upon her; for breaking forth into a clattering and incoherent eulogy on the place and its appointments, she ended breathlessly with the words *elegant-gorgeous*.

One of the most active agencies engaged in the degradation of our language is the style adopted by many reporters and correspondents for the press. It is not the stage only that possesses the fellow that tears a passion to tatters, to very rags.

The fault, however, is not wholly chargeable to these writers; part of it lies at the door of *their* public. The writers know—who, indeed, generally know so well?—what will please the majority of their patrons. Yet, not in every case, not in the greater number of cases, is this style adopted to please them. It is often the result—tolerated, if not countenanced, by many newspapers—of allowing *employés* to make the most, in *space*, of every subject on which they write;

3

to dwell on petty details; to indulge in trite, philosophical reflections; until the reader, in despair, mentally exclaims, "When shall I come to the point?"

One species of this composition was called in a late number of 'The Saturday Review,' tail-lashing. The youthful reporter is represented as a lion, which, having secured a precious morsel of something, it matters not what, takes it aside and gnaws and rends it, with growls and lashings of the tail. The awed spectators are to understand that this lion has a precious morsel, so precious that no lion ever had such a one; and, moreover, that this identical lion is the only one which could do adequate justice to its dissection.

Such a writer is by a grain of sand reminded of a desert; by a mouse, of the fur-trade. The subject having been chosen by him, or suggested to his mind by an occurrence, or forced on his attention by the revelation of a crime,—in any case, in all cases,—he opens the floodgates of his erudition, and deluges it with words. He "rides in the whirlwind, and directs the storm."

Another species of this composition is over-laden with petty and often incongruous details, in the statement of the simplest matters of fact. If even poor John Smith's house catches afire, and the fire is put out in a few minutes :—" Last evening, flames were discovered issuing from the portal of the residence of our respected fellow-citizen, John Smith, Esq. The firemen, with their usual alacrity, were promptly on the spot. The street was soon a scene of wild commotion and uproar, which, with the devouring element, formed a *toute ensemble* of grandeur and subli-mity. The *coup d'œil* soon became truly mag-nificent, the flames having reached a small wood-en shanty, next door, in which was confined a remarkably fine poodle belonging to Mr. Simp-kins, the grocer opposite, favourably known to the public for his superior article of teas, whose howls awakened the sympathies of the by-standers."*

* The introduction of petty details often results in the blundering exhibited; in which the *coup d'œil* is de-scribed as magnificent, when a shanty catches afire, and the howls of *teas* awaken sympathy.

Another species of composition is in great favour with reporters, and with some of "our own correspondents" who write from watering-places, and consists chiefly of slang terms, stereotyped phrases, and trite quotations. A man is a *biped*. A woman is a *feminine*. A child is a *juvenile*. A dog is a *canine*. Fingers are *digits*. Feet are *pedal extremities*. Oysters are *bivalves*. A ball is a *hop*, where "all went merry as a marriage-bell," while the guests "tripped it on the light fantastic toe," * and did not separate until "the wee small hours ayont the twal." † If a hotel-keeper is merely civil, he is "Mr. So-and-so, the gentlemanly proprietor." A ball was "*the* hop of the season." "The Ladies (God bless them!), were lovely"—"the *élite* and fashion"—"fair women and brave men"—"revelry by night"—"banquet-hall deserted." Fill up the spaces, and you will have such a letter, and perhaps many such letters are written on that plan.

* The original is :—

"Come, and trip it, as you go,
On the light fantastic toe."

† The original is :—"Some wee short hour ayont the twal."

In many theatrical criticisms, such a farrago of nonsense, foreign words, foreign phrases, puffery, fustian, never was strung together until these latter-days.

The employment of a foreign word in conversation, or in writing, is legitimate only when the writer has no equivalent in his own language. Why should *we* employ foreign words when we have equivalents in our language? Why, generally, do *our* dramatic critics speak of an actor, or an actress, as an *artiste?* Why do they call the part of an actor, or an actress, a *rôle?* There is for using the word *répertoire* the valid excuse that we have nothing to substitute for it, except a paraphrastic expression; but what excuse can there be for using the words *artiste* and *rôle*, instead of our words, *actor* and *actress*, and *part?*

Lately, there appeared a "theatrical notice" commencing thus:—"The Academy of Music was crowded last evening with an *élite* and intelligent audience," etc. Here is a liberty! *Élite*, which is a noun, is transformed into an adjective by the writer of the notice.

There is another ridiculous thing generally coupled with the use of French words in our newspapers. Not every journal possesses type with the French accents, or has compositors familiar with the accents. In consequence of this, French words which have accents generally appear shorn of those necessary adjuncts. The words, without appropriate accents, are not French, any more than our English "*i*" is "*i*," without the dot, or our English "*t*" is "*t*," without the cross. *Répertoire* and *rôle*, written, or printed, without their appropriate accents, are eyesores to persons familiar with French.

The mania for introducing foreign words, and especially French words, into English composition, renders itself ridiculous in a third way. The words are seldom even spelled correctly. Whether this originates with the writers, or with the compositors, is of little consequence—the words are wrong in print. Compositors often receive blame for what they are not responsible. In certain articles, they cannot be in fault; for, in those, the writers always correct their "proofs."

If a writer uses words with which he is not conversant, whether with respect to their meaning,

their spelling, or their accentuation, the reason
for his failure in all of these particulars is obvi-
ous; but what shall we think of his failure to employ correctly foreign words and phrases so
common that they are met with every day?

In many cases, we see printed in newspapers,
aye! in books too, *hors du combat*, and *esprit
du corps*. Yet, the simple preposition *de*, not the
combined preposition and definite article—*du*, is
to be found in all similar phrases in the French
language.

The French word *sobriquet* is frequently mis-
spelled *soubriquet;* but this is not calculated to
change its pronunciation materially.

What has been said on this head, does not
impugn our right to anglicize words as we
please. If the French take the liberty of calling beef-steak, *bifteck*, and roast-beef, *rosbif*, as
they do; they cannot take umbrage at our dis-
figuring many of the words which we introduce
into our language from theirs. But the cases
of errors cited are not parallel to these, do not
admit of this defence; for the best English usage
—in which the writer includes American—is to
write *esprit de corps, hors de combat, sobriquet*.

The French word *matériel* is frequently used for the French word *personnel.* A few weeks ago, under the head of "Sacred Concerts on Sunday Evenings," appeared the following sentence: —"Again, all of our first-class churches would be comparatively deserted, except for the attraction of the well-trained and talented choirs engaged by them, and, even among the most orthodox members of our churches of all denominations, the *matériel* of the choir is considered as only second in importance to an eloquent and popular pastor." *

During the Rebellion, the writer took to a newspaper an article in which he described what constitutes good troops; using, in that connection, the word *material,* in the sense with which we speak of the *stuff* that a man is made of—meaning his manly qualities. To the editor's objection to the word *material,* the writer did not demur, for it had been loosely employed, but he remonstrated against the the editor's substitution of the French word *matériel;* inasmuch as that word, when relating to armies, distinctively signifies all the *appliances* used by them, guns, waggons, everything, just as the French word *personnel,* when relating to armies, distinctively signifies all the *persons* composing them. Demonstration and remonstrance were alike unavailing; and, with a sense of comfort that at least

There is a very common error in the arrangement of the words in a favourite Latin quotation, which generally appears in print as "*id omne genus*," whereas, it should be "*id genus omne.*" This error cannot possibly be ascribed to compositors.

his name was not to be appended to the article, he committed it to the editorial hands. The following day it appeared in print, and, as he had expected and feared, one of the constituents of good troops was described as their *matériel.*

CHAPTER IV.

INDELICACY.

In the avoidance of certain proper words, and the substitution of other words for them, there is involved the admission of the existence of an indelicate thought. This practice, originating in the prurience of some people's imaginations, has, unhappily, so influenced many worthy people, that even they have contracted the habit of this avoidance, which they have the folly to consider an evidence of refinement.

"A nice man," says Dean Swift, "is a man of nasty ideas;" an apophthegm which conveys a keen satire. So far is it from being true, that the practice mentioned is delicate, it is the height of indelicacy.

An Englishman, to whom an American woman should say, "I have the rheumatism in one of my limbs," might inquire, "Which?" if he did not happen to know that many women in this country, in speaking of their sex's legs to persons of the

other sex, call them distinctively *limbs*, and there
drop the subject, although they might not drop
their skirts a hair's breadth : such is consistency
in the matter of legs.

At a hotel, the writer heard a *lady* direct a
waiter to bring her the *trotter* of a chicken.   He
once met another who was all ankle to the waist,
and all waist to the shoulders.   Happening to
converse with the latter regarding the relative
symmetry of our countrywomen in different parts
of the United States, she, wishing to express her
belief that New England women, of whom she
was one, had as delicately shaped limbs—by which
the writer means arms as well as legs—as the
women of other sections have, stammered out
that they had very fine—ah–ah–ah—extremities.
It is a shame that excellent words, which are a
part of our language, and which served our ances-
tors for hundreds of years, should be driven out of
familiar use by prurient imaginations.   Cock and
Hen are generic names, distinguishing the male
and the female of all kinds of birds ; but The Cock
and The Hen are the distinctive appellations of the
barn-door fowls.   Why then should we substitute
rooster for *cock?*   Does not the hen of the same

species roost also? We say *woodcock, peacock, weathercock,*—although some persons object even to these,— why, then, should we not use the distinctive name from which the compounds are derived? One would suppose that a word which is not obsolete, or quaint, which was and is good enough in a translation of the Scriptures, would be good enough for every-day use. Or shall we read, where Peter denies the Master—"the *rooster* crew?"

The word *rooster* is an Americanism, which, the sooner we forget, the better; not because it is an Americanism, but because the use of it, as is also the case in the other words criticised in this place, has an effect the very reverse of that alleged to be intended.

In our translation of the Scriptures we read of an animal called The Ass. In the moral tales, entitled The Fables of Æsop, we read of the same animal, also called The Ass. But, in much modern speech and writing, the ass has become the donkey.

Now, although a donkey must be either an *ass* or a *mule,* neither an ass nor a mule is necessarily a donkey. An ass may be a wild-ass, or an unbroken domestic one, and so may a mule be either wild, or unbroken. A donkey is an ass, or a mule, *broken to the saddle, or to draught.* The word, on account of which this is avoided, is not the same in derivation, spelling, or pronunciation.

The length to which this spurious delicacy has proceeded in this country would astonish many who have given in their adherence to some of these affectations. The writer has visited and resided in many parts of it, and can vouch, from personal observation, for what he affirms. Among some country-people, he once accidentally discovered, to his surprise, that the children had been taught to call pismires, *antmires.* On one occasion, to his knowledge, when some little girls from the city were spending their summer-vacation at a farm-house, one of them, happening to speak of her being afraid of a bull in the neighbourhood, was frowned out of countenance by the mistress of the house, who, taking her aside, chid her for using the word, telling her that it was *indecent.*

It is a suggestive fact, that wherever education and refinement most prevail, there is the least of this practice. In witnessing cases of it, there often comes into the mind of the writer the reply which a French teacher of his acquaintance once made to a female pupil, who, at recitation, hesitated to pronounce the word *leg*, where it occurred in an account of the wounding of Napoleon :— "*Ah, Mademoiselle, la vraie délicatesse ne pense pas à de telles choses.*" True delicacy has no such ideas.

It is a poor surgeon that, wishing to extirpate a blemish, scruples to use the knife boldly. With the originators and abettors of this false delicacy rest the responsibility for the need of using it at all.

CHAPTER V.

VULGARISMS CONSISTING IN THE INAPPROPRIATE USE OF WORDS CORRECT IN THEMSELVES.

THERE are some words which, when inappropriately used, although correct in themselves, mark the speaker as ill-educated and underbred.

The titles *gentleman* and *lady* are most seldom on the lips of those who have the best right to be dignified by them. Gentlemen and ladies assert their right to the distinction by their demeanour, not by arrogating to themselves the titles.

What constitutes propriety in the use of these two words can be determined by discussing one of them, for to each is applicable all that can be said of the other. Let us therefore choose for consideration the rather more misused word, *lady*.

By common courtesy, ladies comprise all women who conduct themselves with propriety, and possess certain conventional manners. In one's heart of hearts, however, one knows that all these are not ladies. Each person has some criterion by which to distinguish those who are from those who are not.

The object here is not to discuss what constitutes a lady, but to define when the title which belongs to the character is appropriately used, and when misused. Granting, in any particular case, the right to the distinction, the title is not always properly employed. For instance, were one speaking of the admirable traits of character possessed by a female acquaintance, it would be incorrect for one to say, " She is a fine lady." One should, in that case, say, " She is a fine woman." A fine woman is something infinitely superior to a fine lady. The works of Fielding abound in fine ladies, but they are not often fine women. In the case supposed, the term *fine* belongs to the idea of sex, not to that of station.

Again, if one should wish to speak of the wit of a female acquaintance, it would be incorrect to say, " She is a witty lady." Wit, or any other attribute of the mind, does not belong distinctively to ladies, nor even to their sex, but to individual men and women. The same observation applies when education and learning are concerned.

Were one to say of a certain person, "She is a well-dressed lady," the expression would imply that ladies may not be well-dressed; which is not a fact, taste in dress being a characteristic of a lady, its appropriateness to occasion being its marked excellence: whereas a vulgar woman always supposes that she is well-dressed when she is much-dressed, and, in consequence, is generally overdressed.

Thousands of cases might be cited, in which the word is misused; as, when a person speaks of a good lady, a modest lady, a charitable lady, an amiable lady, a handsome lady, a graceful lady. In some of them the expression is wrong because the epithet is involved in the character; and in others it is wrong because the epithet is applied to individuals as belonging to the female sex, not as restricted to those who are ladies.

On inquiry's being made at a house for Mrs. ——, she sometimes introduces herself thus:— "I am the lady." She should say either, "I am Mrs.——," or else, "I am the person." One who uses either of these expressions might be

4

the *lady* of the house; using the first one, she could not possibly be, although she might be the *mistress* of it.

A lady instinctively shrinks from a direct, personal announcement of station. Only in rare cases can she be forced to make it. To an intimate friend, with whom she feels safe from the suspicion of vulgarity, she might say, or imply, on an occasion when warranted by the subject, that she is a lady. Thus, for example:—"The passengers consisted chiefly of rough, noisy people, among whom I, of course, could not feel comfortable." Or, she tells Mrs.——, positively, that she can have nothing to do with the proceeding of writing their complaints in an anonymous note to their pastor. Mrs.——answers, "why not?" "Because," returns she, mortified and insulted at Mrs.——'s supposing her capable of the act, "I am a lady." Here is an extreme case—that of a person driven in self-defence to make, in one word, an announcement of her sentiments.

All expressions which involve a claim to personal distinction should be scrupulously avoided. Any woman can say, when referring to the tenderness of heart possessed by her in common with her sex, "I have the feelings of a *woman;*" because she confesses to the possession of a characteristic *accorded* to the whole sex. But if she says, "I have the feelings of a *lady*," she singles herself out, by conferring on herself a title of distinction. No woman of delicacy—*lady*, can do that.

A form of vulgarity in using the word *lady* is very common in advertisements :—"Wanted, a first-class saleslady,"—"Wanted, a situation as saleslady," etc. Undoubtedly, a woman who sells may be a lady, but she is not one *because* she sells. She is a sales*woman*, the correlative of salesman. What should we say, if the latter styled himself a salesgentleman? The proper form for these advertisements is this :—"Wanted, a saleswoman,—Wanted, a situation as saleswoman,—Wanted, a situation as salesman."

As an evidence of the loss of significance resulting from undiscriminating use of the titles under consideration, take the majority of advertisements in which they appear, and do we not often see such as this?—"Boarding: Two respectable young ladies can find home comforts in a private family," etc. As if ladies could be other than respectable! Even in a leading editorial of a newspaper remarkable for its general ability, accuracy, and good taste, there lately appeared these phrases: "every well-bred gentleman,"—"every well-bred lady." As if, in either sex, to be well-bred, is not to be either a gentleman or a lady! as if to be a gentleman or a lady, is not to be well-bred!

The introduction of the word *lady* into advertisements sometimes leads to ludicrous readings of the subject-matter, as in the following instance, which the writer noticed a few years ago:—"Wanted, by a young lady with a fine breast of milk, a situation as wet-nurse;" by which phraseology was suggested to every reader's mind an idea foreign to the advertiser's thought, and, probably, to the truth.

The expressions, "my gentleman-friend,"—"my lady-friend," are vulgarisms. The presumption is, when a gentleman or a lady speaks of any one as being his or her friend, that it *must* be a lady, if a woman, and a gentleman, if a man. The *station* is taken for granted, and, generally, it is not necessary to specify the *sex*. When necessary to do so, the object should be accomplished by mentioning the *name* of the person, in connection with the word, *friend*. This may be done in three forms. First. My friend, Mr. (Mrs., Miss)——. Second. A friend of mine, Mr. (Mrs., Miss)——. Third. Mr. (Mrs., Miss)——, a friend of mine.

When it is necessary to distinguish friends as divisible into the sexes, the proper expressions to employ are, "my male friends,"—"my female friends."

What can be a greater vulgarity than a man's inquiring after the health of another's wife, thus:—"How is your Lady?" or than a man's entering his and his wife's name on a Hotel-Register, as Mr. So-and-so and Lady?*

In England, *Lady* is a title corresponding to *Lord*. In this country, it is not a title, except by courtesy. My Lord So-and-so, travelling with his Lady, is known to be travelling with his *wife*.

---

* A vulgarity of the same sort is common in France. There, a gentleman always says, *ma femme* (my wife), but the vulgar, through affectation, often say, *mon épouse* (my spouse).

An untitled man travelling with his *Lady* is in a very equivocal position. A gentleman without rank, if accompanied by his wife, puts his name on a Hotel-Register, as Mr.——and *wife*.

It is impossible to specify every case in which the terms *gentleman* and *lady* should be avoided, and every case in which they should be employed. The rule which one can deduce from the principles discussed, is, that as regards one's own personality, there should be an entire avoidance of them in self-application, and as regards others, an avoidance of them, *when they are not required as part of the language of courtesy, nor as referring to the distinctive traits appertaining to the stations.**

---

* The only exceptions are in the case of youth and of age. It is customary, in speaking *of* well-grown boys and girls of a certain station, to call them "young gentlemen" and "young ladies." It is also customary, in speaking *of* old men and old women of a certain station, to call them "old gentlemen" and "old ladies." An additional epithet is frequently applied to them, as when we speak of "a fine old gentleman,"—"a fine old lady,"—"a nice old gentleman,"—"a nice old lady."—"a cross old gentleman,"—"a cross old lady."

Moreover, there can be no verbal qualification of the terms, although there may be mental qualification of them. A gentleman is a gentleman, and a lady is a lady, irrespective of their position in the world. The elements are intrinsic. Therefore it is vulgar to say, " a first-class lady,"— "very much of a lady,"—or to speak in the same strain of a gentleman. In each sex, persons worthy of the titles exhibit individual differences, being various in nature, birth, intellect, education, beauty, elegance, accomplishments, fortune; but some of these possessions are accessory, not essential, to the composition of the lady and the gentleman. They add lustre to, but they cannot constitute the characters.

The writer has dwelt at some length on this subject, because there is urgent need of reform in it. The undiscriminating use of the terms *gentleman* and *lady* has so prostituted them, that even in cases where they might with propriety be used, they are often shunned by the refined. We should take warning from the fate of *genteel*, a word so much abused at one time that, among refined people, it has become almost obsolete. It never became so offensive to ears polite as the words last mentioned, for the reason that it never received the self-application which is fast rendering those words obnoxious. It was, however, applied so indiscriminately as to occasion disgust. There was not only a genteel man, or a genteel woman, but there were genteel hands, feet, noses, smiles, coaches, hats, gloves, boots, shawls, cloaks, genteel any thing and every thing.

It is strange that the persons who are most addicted to the use of the word *lady*, are also the very ones who do not scruple to apply the word *female* to every degree of womankind. Yet, the words *male* and *female* are not properly used as *nouns*, except in speaking of the lower animals. To the sexes of mankind, they are properly applied only as *adjectives*. We can say:—the male pupils, the female pupils, the male singers, the female singers, the male descendants, the female descendants, and so on; but we cannot say of a man, "He is a handsome male." But, is it any better to say of a woman, "She is a handsome female?" We often hear, and read, that a church, or other building, was crowded with *females*; that "the *females* of the

Rev.——'s congregation take much interest
in the approaching Fair."* This is detestable!
Let us speak of the whole range of beasts, birds,
and fishes, as males and females; but let us not
derogate from our dignity. There are no words
nobler than *man* and *woman*, not even the words
gentleman and *lady*. The former and the latter
have different spheres, and are not interchangeable terms.

When describing mixed public assembly, it is
in better taste to use the terms *ladies* and *gentlemen*, than to speak of *males* and *females*. But

* The name " Female Institute " is incorrect. A sing-
er, a descendant, and others, may be *female*. But,
whether we mean to characterize an institution, or to characterize merely the building which it occupies, we cannot
with propriety use the word *female*. Houses and institutions are of the neuter gender. The only possible con-
structions that the name " Female Institute" will bear are
the following :—A house of the feminine gender, an institution of the feminine gender, or a house for females—
the last construction being the least in accordance with
the literal reading of the words. " Women's Institute,"—
" Girls' Institute,"—are the best names by which to designate Institutions for women and girls, and next to them
come the names, " Ladies' Institute,"—" Young Ladies'
Institute."

it is in far better taste to say *men* and *women;* especially, and from a higher motive than good taste, when we refer, however distantly, to divine worship.

CHAPTER VI.

VULGARISMS CONSISTING IN THE CONTRACTION OF WORDS.

THE words which were discussed in the last chapter are legitimate words when legitimately used. We now come to the consideration of several contractions, which have not reached the dignity of being recognized as parts of our language.

As remarked in the last chapter, the title of *gentleman* is most seldom on the lips of those who have the best right to the designation. When, however, they do have occasion to employ the word, they do so without contracting it. *Gents* may serve well enough for the signs of " Gentlemen's Furnishing Stores," or for the speech of hackney-coachmen, but it is inadmissible in the language of good society.

From the Italian words, singular and plural, *pantalone, pantaloni*, we received through the French people—through whom we received the

garment also—our word *pantaloons*. The word
has been anglicized in this form ; written and
spelled thus, it preserves the sign of its derivation ; it is easy to pronounce ; and it is not un-
euphonious. In fact, there can be no objection
to it. Why, then, is it ever contracted into
pants ? One's time must be precious if one
contracts words to save it. *Pants*, as well as
gents, will do well enough for signs, and among
the uneducated ; but, in the conversation or in
the writing of the educated and refined, the word
should be eschewed. *Trousers*, or *pantaloons*,
is the proper name of the garment in question.

Kids is another vile contraction. Habit blinds
people to the unseemliness of a term like this.
How would it sound if one should speak of silk
gloves as *silks*

There was some excuse, on account of the
length of the names, for contracting into *gum-
elastics, india-rubbers*, and *rubbers*, the original
names for gum shoes—*india-rubber shoes*, or
gum-elastic shoes ; but there is no excuse for contracting the present name *gum shoes* into *gums*.

We derive from the French language our word
chemise—pronounced *shemmeeze*. In French, the

word denotes a man's shirt, as well as the under-garment worn by women. In this country, it is often pronounced by people who should know better—*shimmy*. The word is degraded by this pronunciation, is as different in sound from the true word, as different in associations, as *fiddle* is from *violin* and from *its* associations. A lady invariably pronounces it *shemmeeze*. Rather than call it *shimmy*, resume the use of the old English words, *shift* and *smock*.

The writer will forestall the captious critic, by remarking that he is well aware of the word's not being used in public; and will add, that it matters not, inasmuch as the language of the refined is not laid aside in private.

That good usage does occasionally tolerate contractions has been admitted by the act of producing some of them. Whether it is or is not justifiable in making exceptions is of no consequence in enabling us to arrive at a conclusion which shall guide our practice. The question as to the propriety of any given contraction is always one of fact as to its being authorized by good usage; and although, of course, there must sometimes be difference of opinion as to what, in a particular case, good usage dictates, there can be no final appeal, as, in the case of the construction of sentences, may be made to grammar. In this matter, as well as in pronunciation, the decision of good usage is final. It unqualifiedly condemns *gents*, *pants*, *kids*, *gums*, and *shimmy* and, as a general rule, other contractions.

CHAPTER VII.

VULGARISMS CONSISTING IN USING WORDS IN A WRONG SENSE.

A very prevalent error in the use of a word in a wrong sense is to be found in the expression, "our mutual friend." It is to be regretted that Dickens has contributed to give currency to this phrase, by calling his last novel, 'Our Mutual Friend,' without adding one word, in the book itself, to indicate that its title is an incorrect expression. The presumption is that he did not believe the phrase to be erroneous. Yet the most correct speakers and writers unite in condemning it, Macaulay stigmatizing it as a "low vulgarism."

Primarily, the word *mutual* relates to persons, and to two persons only. The idea that it conveys is reciprocity of sentiment or of action. Two persons may have a *mutual* affection or a *mutual* aversion, but how can a third person participate in *that* affection, or in *that* aversion?

Two persons may *mutually* embrace, but they cannot mutually embrace *some one else*. Individually, every human being partakes of the lot of *mutual* dependence. Secondarily, the word may refer to many persons regarded as comprised in two divisions. The intercourse of two societies may be for their *mutual* advantage. Secondarily, and figuratively, the word relates to numbers of any things holding relations with each other. The arts show *mutual* dependence. But in none of these cases does the word signify possession. If people casting aside the idea of the sentiment uniting two persons supposed to be able to use the phrase, "our mutual friend," are reconciled to its signifying merely joint possession of another friend, why may they not also adopt the phrases, "our mutual business," or, "our mutual house?"

Our *common* friend, *common* enemy, *common* acquaintance, or whatever the case may be, are the proper expressions—meaning, the friend, enemy, acquaintance, *common* to both of us—our friend, enemy, acquaintance, *in common*.*

* A Life Assurance Company of the United States publishes 'Our Mutual Friend,' a newspaper, the motto of

The word *party* is now frequently used as synonymous with *man*, and is daily growing in favour.   The use of it in this sense is quite ancient, but never became common until of late years.   The present use of it in this sense is so general as to seem to originate in some particular affection for it.   It is a pet word.

This corruption has proceeded from the word in its signification of joint concern in any act; a meaning with which it is properly used in Law, where it so frequently occurs, that the people, having become habituated to it in its technical sense, adopted it, and conferred on it an additional meaning.

It is very natural that this should have happened; for, if two persons were the parties to a marriage, or other contract, if two or more persons were parties to a suit at law, or to proceedings of any sort requiring combination or opposition, each of these persons was *a party* to that in which he or she was concerned.   Hence the word came to be used to designate a single

which is, " Ignorance is the curse of God, knowledge the wing whereby we fly to Heaven."

5

individual, and, not only that, but strictly, a *man.*⌉

But it should not be associated with the idea of a single person, irrespectively of that person's relations with another, or with other persons. If, with a meaning restricted to designating a single person irrelatively to other persons, it were applied not only to men, but to women, it would be objectionable; but, as the case stands, it is doubly objectionable, on the score that it is not philosophically applied, as for mere consistency's sake it should be, equally to men and to women.

It is not uncommon to hear persons who do not weigh their words, say:—"I just met a *party* from New York, who came on with a *party* consisting of several wealthy *parties*." Here we have a legitimate meaning of the word *party*— expressive of social assembly—used in connection with the word with its illegitimate meaning; and, as we constantly have occasion to speak of one man as well as of men in company with each other, the use of the same word for both ideas is creative of confusion in the mind. Why is it not better to say, "I met a man," or, "I met a gentleman," or, "I met a person;" instead of saying, "I met a party?"   Is the word *party* a particularly sweet morsel to roll around the tongue?

Lest the writer be suspected of having set up a man of straw, for the greater facility with which it could be toppled over, he quotes, suppressing names, the following account of a late distressing railroad accident, rendered, by the mode of narration, almost ludicrous :—

.   .   .   .   .   "Several other *parties* were quite badly, though not dangerously, injured by the shock which resulted from the collision.

" The scene at the place of the accident was most heart-rending.   We learn that the screams of the unfortunate *parties* in the sleeping-car, previous to their death, were beyond all description.   However, nothing could save them ; the flames spread on every hand, and to move was as certain death as to remain in the berths ; but a few moments only sufficed to end the terrible agonies of the unfortunate *parties ;* and save with respect to the unknown female from ——, little else is left than the ashes of the doomed ones.   .   .   .   .   .   .

" We learn that one of the sisters —— reached the door of the car, and broke the window, but was unable to obtain an egress. Her situation was observed by other *parties*, and an axe was procured from the train, and an effort made to relieve her ; but while the *party* was attempting to batter down the door of the car, a sudden burst of flames struck her, and she fell dead." . . . .

Individual is another word frequently used in a wrong sense, or rather, restricted to meaning only a *man ;* whereas it is applicable as well to every human being, although it is seldom used in reference to persons not adults. It may be applied to beasts; as, for instance, a naturalist may speak of "an individual of any species of the brute creation."   It may be applied even to the lowest and the most minute forms of animal life.

The use of the word in the restricted sense mentioned is a vulgarism.   Yet this use of it is quite common in the United States, and Dean Alford says, is quite common in England.

As an adjective, the word sometimes has duty to do which no other word can perform.   If, for instance, a traveller, looking from a mountain towards a distant city, could see each one of the houses, he could not otherwise communicate the fact so well as by saying that he could "distinguish the *individual* houses." This use of the word as an adjective, will give an idea of its proper application as a noun, as which it means each and every living creature, although it is applied especially to men and women.

CHAPTER VIII.

VULGARISMS CONSISTING IN THE MISPRONUNCIA-
TION OF ANGLICIZED WORDS.

IT has previously been remarked that a foreign word is not to be tolerated when an equivalent can be found in one's own language. It may be added that, when a foreign word *is* introduced into any language, it should be received and retained with its original spelling and pronunciation as much as possible unimpaired.

This process, which in our language is termed anglicizing, was effected in the case of the following words, all originally in correct and daily use, but now fast settling into apparently irremediable corruption.

The French word *amateur*—correctly pronounced *ammatur*—is often called *ammachoor*. It is as easy to say *ammatur* as it is to say *ammachoor*, and the corruption in the pronunciation probably originated in people's seeing the word's final syllable spelled *teur*, and presuming that it

was to be pronounced as we, in English, pronounce *ture*, whereas *teur*, in French, is always
pronounced *tur*.*

The French word *connoisseur*—old French,
modern French, *connaisseur*—was anglicized with
that form when it was so spelled in France. Its
last syllable is pronounced *sur*, and the whole
word, *konnessur*—not *konnayshoor* and *konnay-
seer*, as it is frequently mispronounced.

The French word *bouquet* has been adopted
by us, with its spelling and its pronunciation unchanged ; yet it is frequently printed *boquet*,
and pronounced *bo*-kay. The true pronunciation
is boo-*kay*, which is just as easy to say as
bo-kay. Where is to be found the authority for
changing the spelling and the pronunciation of
this word ? Both Webster and Worcester write
it *bouquet*, and pronounce it boo-*kay ;* and the
English lexicographers do likewise.†

The French words *Deux Temps*, although they
have not yet found their way into our diction-

* Even the English syllable *ture* does not give the
sound of *choor*.

† Webster and Worcester give also the pronunciation
boo-kay. That given in the text is the correct one. In

aries, may, on account of the popularity of the waltz well known by that name, be considered anglicized. They are pronounced *Durh Tongh*, and mispronounced *Dew Ton*.

The French word *début*—correctly pronounced *day-bu*—is often called de-*but*. An actor, or an actress, is sometimes said to have de*but*ted. The latter, however, is not the usual error, but the coining of a word. In France, an actor, or an actress, can make his or her *début* (day-bu), or can *début* (day-bu); because the French have a verb, *débuter* (day-bu-tay), meaning to make one's first appearance on the stage, or elsewhere in public.

The French word *étagère*, meaning the shelves for nicknacks, so frequently seen in parlours, is correctly pronounced *a-tahj-ayre*, and incorrectly pronounced *a-tahjer*.

The French word *ruche*, correctly pronounced *rewsh*, means *beehive*, from which—

French, there is no accent in the sense with which we speak of accent, and as the second syllable of the word *bouquet*, as represented by *kay*, can be pronounced either long or short, the effect of laying stress on the first syllable, which is always long, is to make the word sound thus—*boo*-keh.

probably on account of the resemblance between the plaits of blondlace and the cells of the honey-comb—is named the delicate quilling used by women, sometimes inserted on the inside edge of the bonnet, sometimes serving as an ornamental covering for the throat, and sometimes as a trimming for ball dresses. This word is incorrectly called *rouge*, the pronunciation and the use of which are very well known.

The French word *savant* is, in the plural, *savans*—not *savants*, as we frequently see it printed. The word, in the singular number, is correctly pronounced *savvonh ;* in the plural, *savvonhs*.

La Fayette—anglicized *Lafayette*—is correctly pronounced *Laf-fi-yet*, and often mispronounced *Laffyet*, sometimes *Layfyet*. These vulgar pronunciations have been so often criticized, they should be much less common than they are. The most devoted foreign friend of Washington, and of the United States, deserves better at our hands than to be known as *Laffyet*, or *Layfyet*.

The Italian word *piano* is correctly pronounced *peanno*—not pi-anno, nor pianner. The third is the lowest-known pronunciation; the second, although only a grade above it, is entitled to the mention of that distinction.

From the Latin word *nubes*, signifying a cloud, we take the name of *The Nube*,* or *The Cloud*, the hood of zephyr worsted, often worn by women for a head-dress in the streets at night. The name is very expressive, owing to the light, fleecy appearance of the hood. When, within a few years, this head-dress came into fashion—for zephyr worsteds, it would seem, are a modern invention—it was called *The Nube*. As soon, however, as the wearing of it became so general that instead of being as formerly knit, it was generally woven by manufacturers, and sold in large numbers, its name was corrupted into *Nubia*. The pasteboard boxes in which it was sent to market were always marked, *Nubias*. This labelling, and the resulting mispronunciation of the word by most saleswomen who disposed of the article, were by many people regarded as high authority for the spelling and the pronunciation of the word, and, doubtless, have been the chief agencies in its corruption.

* Pronounced *nu'be*.

For the sake of precision, those of the preceding words which in the originals have accents have been so marked. But, as those words have been anglicized, they do not ordinarily require either accents or italicizing. They are a part of our language.

When it is said of a word, that it has been adopted from another language, with its spelling and its pronunciation unchanged,—as was remarked of the word *bouquet*,—the statement is not strictly true with regard to its pronunciation. There is, belonging to every language, an accent, a complexional character which pervades the whole of it; and this no foreigner can acquire, although some persons do fondly imagine that they have succeeded in the endeavour.

CHAPTER IX.

GRAMMATICAL ERRORS.*

THIS chapter must begin with a defence of its title.

The correctness of the expression "grammatical errors" has been disputed. "How," it has been asked, "can an error be grammatical?" How, it may be replied, can we with propriety say, "grammatically incorrect?" Yet we can do so.

No one will question the propriety of saying, "grammatically correct." Yet the expression is the acknowledgment of the existence of things "grammatically *in*correct." Likewise, the phrase "grammatical correctness" implies the existence of "grammatical *in*correctness." If, then, a sentence is "grammatically incorrect," or, what is the same thing, has "grammatical incorrectness," it includes a *grammatical error*. "Grammatically incorrect," signifies *incorrect*

* Vulgarisms and other errors.

with relation to the rules of grammar. "Grammatical errors," signifies *errors with relation to the rules of grammar.*

They who ridicule the phrase " grammatical errors," and substitute the phrase "errors in grammar," make an egregious mistake. Can there, it may be asked with some show of reason, be an error in grammar? Why, grammar is a science founded in our nature, referable to our ideas of time, relation, method; imperfect, doubtless, as to the system by which it is represented; but surely we cannot speak of error in that which is error's criterion! All this is hypercritical, but hypercriticism must be met with its own weapons.

Of the two expressions, "a grammatical error," and "an error in grammar," the former is preferable. If one's judgment can accept neither, one must relinquish the belief in the possibility of tersely expressing the idea of an offence against grammatical rules. Indeed, it would be difficult to express the idea even by circumlocution. Should some one say, "This sentence is, according to the rules of grammar, incorrect." "What!" the hypercritic may exclaim, "incorrect! and according to the rules of grammar!" "This sentence, then," the corrected person would reply, "contains an error in grammar." "Nonsense!" the hypercritic may shout, "grammar is a science; you may be wrong in its interpretation, but principles are immutable!"

After this, it need scarcely be added that, grammatically, no one can make a mistake, that there can be no grammatical mistake, that there can be no bad grammar, and, consequently, no bad English: a very pleasant conclusion which would save us a great amount of trouble if it did not lack the insignificant quality of being true.

A verb used as if governing the nominative case of a personal pronoun.

"Let's you and I go."

One person says to another, or to others, "Let us go;" never, "let *we* go." The very same mistake, however, is often concealed from him when he resolves *us* into its component ideas,—*you* and *I*,—and says, "Let's you and I go." Yet the word *I* has, as he very well knows, another form —*me*. This form—the objective case, the same case in which *us* and *you* are—must be used, and he should say, " Let you and *me* go ;" for *let's* also is incorrect, being the contraction of *let us*, and therefore a repetition of *you* and *me*, thus—"Let us you and me go," which is absurd.

A preposition used as if governing the nominative case of personal pronouns. (No. 1.)

" Between you and I," etc.

An error, even more common than the preceding one, occurs in the expressions, "Between you and I,"—"Between you and he (or she),"—"Between you and they." Here, *I, he, she, they*, in the nominative case, should be in the objective case—*me, him, her, them.* The expressions are therefore correct thus :—" Between you and me,"—" Between you and him (or her), "—" Between you and them."

A preposition used as if governing the nominative case of personal pronouns. (No. 2.)

" From he who," etc.

The phrase "from he who" is sometimes spoken, but oftener written, owing to the fact that the sentences in which it occurs are seldom used in conversation ; as, "We expect most from *he who* has had most advantages." The person who speaks or writes such a sentence imagines that the relative pronoun *who* cannot refer to *him*, or *her* (me, us, them), but must always refer to *he*, or *she* (I, we, they), or to the nouns which these words may represent.

We cannot say from *I*, from *he*, from *she*, from *we*, from *they*. The two following sentences exhibit the proper combinations:—"We expect most from *him*, or *her* (them) who has (have) had most advantages." "Expect nothing from *me* (us) who am (are) too poor to bestow."

Remember that the word *that* is sometimes a mere substitute for *who* or *which*, and then examine the following sentences :—"Visiting the iniquity of the fathers upon the children, unto the third and fourth generation of *them that* hate me : And shewing mercy unto thousands to *them that* love me, and keep my commandments."

A few weeks ago the writer met with this sentence in print:—"Ought we to esteem the man who faces danger, or he who deceives ? Esteem *he !* The last clause should be—"or *him who* deceives."

Personal pronouns used in the objective case, instead of in the nominative case.

"It is me," etc.

The expressions, "It is (was) me,"—"It is (was) him,"—"It is (was) her,"—"It is (was) them,"—are all incorrect. The verb *To Be*, of which *is* and *was* are parts, takes the same case after it as before it. The word *it* is nominative to *is* (was); and *me, him, her, them*, must there-fore be in the nominative case, respectively—*I, he, she, they.*

"It is (was) I,"—"It is (was) he,"—"It is (was) she,"—"It is (was) they," are correct expressions.

We sometimes hear even the gross error of two words in the objective case, used as nomina-tives to a verb; as, " Him and me went." No one ever says, " *Us* went," yet, " Him and me went," is the same mistake; as *him* and *me* are equivalent to *us*—all three being in the objective case, instead of in the nominative case —*he, I, we.* The sentence should be, " He and I went."

Personal pronouns used in the objective case, instead of in the possessive case.

"Him staying," etc.

Me, him, and *them,* the objective cases of the personal pronouns *I, he,* and *they,* are often incorrectly used for the possessive cases, *my, his,* and *their;* as, "I do not like *him* staying out so late at night." The sentence should be, "I do not like *his* staying out so late at night." One sentence expresses an idea entirely different from that expressed by the other. The former states that the person referred to is not liked when staying out late at night, and implies that he *is* liked when *not* staying out late at night. But the liking or the disliking the person cannot depend on his staying out at night, and that is not the idea intended to be expressed. What the speaker dislikes is not the *person* when staying out late at night, but the person's *staying out late at night*—the act.

Whether we should use the word *him,* or *them,* or the word *his,* or *their,* depends upon what idea is intended to be conveyed. "I saw *him* skating," means that I saw him, and he was skating. "I saw *his* skating," means that I saw the quality of his skating. "We heard *them* singing," means that we heard them engaged in the act of singing. "We heard *their* singing," means that our attention was particularly attracted to the singing. "I did not notice *them* passing," means that, as they passed, I took no notice of them. "I did not notice *their* passing," means that their passing escaped my observation.

Her has not been introduced into the preceding examples, because *her* is the possessive case as well as the objective case of *she:* that is to say, more precisely, the possessive case and the objective case have, in this instance, the same *form.*

> A personal pronoun used instead of one of the demonstrative pronouns.

" Them things," etc.

The personal pronoun *them* is frequently used for the demonstrative pronouns *these, those ;* as, "them things,"—"them people,"—"them apples," etc. One might as well say, "him carriage,"—"him store,"—"him nose,"—"me eye,"—"me paper,"—"me pen."

The demonstrative pronouns distinguish between two sets of things, mental, moral, or physical—*these* relating to the more near, *those* to the more remote. *They* is a personal pronoun, and can be prefixed to nouns only when it is in the possessive case—*their;* as, *their* things, *their* apples, etc. We should say, *these* things, *those* things, *these* people, *those* people, *these* apples, *those* apples, etc. ———

A relative as an interrogative pronoun, used in the nominative case, instead of in the objective case.

Who used for *whom.*

"Who did you see?" The error in this sentence will readily be perceived by putting it into another form; thus, "Who saw you?"—the very reverse of what is meant to be said.

Put it into another form, by reversing the last, and it is, "You saw who?" which, if correct, so is, "You saw he?"—"You saw she?" etc. But it is *not* correct. It should be, " *Whom* did you see?" or, " *Whom* saw you?" or, "You saw *whom?*" Turn it as you please, you cannot now change the meaning of the sentence.

A relative pronoun used in the objective case, instead of in the nominative case.

Whom used for *who*.

As in the expression, "Who did you see?" *who* is incorrectly used for *whom*, so, in the following one, *whom* is incorrectly used for *who*.

From a newspaper—such expressions are common in print and in conversation—the following clause is taken :—"For the benefit of those whom she thought were his friends." The error in it can be at once rendered apparent by enclosing in brackets two words which are parenthetical. It then reads :—"For the benefit of those whom [she thought] were his friends. *Whom* were his friends! The wording should be, "*who* she thought were his friends."

Of all the errors heretofore noticed, this is the one which most frequently escapes detection, because parenthetical words conceal it.

A pronoun in the plural number used as if agreeing with an antecedent in the singular number.

"A person—if—they."

It is incorrect to say, "*A person* must be very short-sighted if *they* cannot recognize a friend twenty feet off." Here we have, in the plural, *they*, referring to *a person*. The word *one*

must be substituted for both *a person* and for
they ; thus, " *One* must be very short sighted
if *one* cannot recognize a friend twenty feet off."*

A verb in the singular number used as if agree-
ing with a nominative in the plural number.

"It is one of the subjects that is," etc.

"It is one of the subjects that *is*," etc.   " In
one of the houses that *has*," etc. In sentences
like these, where the word *one* is used, followed by
several words, among the last of which are a noun
in the nominative plural, and its relative pronoun,
nominative to a verb immediately succeeding, it is
quite common to hear the verb put in the singular
number.   In the first example given above, *that*
relates to *subjects,* which is plural, and therefore
requires *are :*—"It is one of the subjects that
are," etc.   In the second example, *that* relates to

* Often we cannot without affectation avoid using the
word *he* as relating to *a person*. It is probable that the
perception of the incongruity resulting from applying a
word indicative of sex to an antecedent not specifying it,
is what has led to the use of the word *they* as a substitute.
A personal pronoun which should be non-committal on the
question of sex would be a great convenience.

houses, which, being plural, requires *have :*—" In one of the houses that *have*," etc.

The examples cited are not at all like the following:—" One of the most important things to be done *is*," etc. In this case, the whole of the preceding clause is regarded as conveying one comprehensive idea, which, represented by the singular number, forms the nominative to the verb *is*. In the sentences above, the pronoun *that*, in both instances, relates to the word immediately preceding it, and takes its plural character from that word.

Violation of good usage with regard to *you* and *were*.

" You was."

"You was" is frequently heard in New England, and, apparently, is gaining ground elsewhere.

Its introduction originated in the reasoning, that, whereas *you* is employed in the singular number, as well as in the plural, when so employed it should not be applied to a verb in the plural. Now we cannot legislate in this way about language. *You* is employed for both the singular number and the plural number, and good usage says that in both it shall have the verb in the plural form—*were.*

It is by no means anomalous for a verb in the plural number to be united with a noun or a pronoun in the singular number. We say, and correctly say:—"If the gardener were to do the transplanting now,"—"If the letter were written,"—"If it were to rain,"—"If I were you," —"If I were going,"—"If he were going." Here are nouns and pronouns, in the singular number, nominatives to a verb in the plural number: a mode reserved for the expression of a certain idea—contingency. To be consistent with *you was,* its advocates would not only have to abolish this subjunctive form of the verb, but also to say, in the verb *To Have,* "You *has,*" in the verb *To Do,* "You *does.*" No one is willing to go quite so far as that, except perhaps the negro-minstrels, who, in one of their burlesques, say, "You am n't;" its being a matter of indifference to them what they say, so that it is laughable.

CHAPTER X.

GRAMMATICAL ERRORS—CONTINUED.*

"I have saw," etc.

MANY persons who do not say "I *done*," and "I *seen*," do say, "I *have saw.*"

This may be evidence of the truth of the hackneyed line from Pope—a little learning is a dangerous thing. Seeing, being a conscious act more continuous than any other that human beings perform, and the recounting of what has been seen forming the staple of most conversation, it happens that in a community where general education is far above saying *I seen*, numbers of persons, having been corrected in it, fall headlong into the error of "I *have saw.*"

The same mistake is apparent in the following item from a late paper: "—— and family *have* arrived in Washington, and *took* (taken) up their quarters for the winter," etc.

* Vulgarisms.—Confusion of tenses.

"*Have went,*" as well as false collocation in other verbs, often escapes notice, owing to the circumstance that one part of the verb is in one clause of a sentence, and one part of it far removed in the other, or in another, if there are more than two clauses; as, "I *have* walked four or five miles, and, although much fatigued, *went* to a dozen places." The same persons who could say this without perceiving the error, would see and use the relation between *have* and *been* in the following similarly constructed, but correct sentence :—"I *have* walked four or five miles, and, although much fatigued, *been* enjoying myself." If this is right, and it is right, the preceding sentence should be, "I *have* walked four or five miles, and, although much fatigued, *gone* to a dozen places."

In a late paper this passage occurs :— "Hold a mirror so that Planet Jupiter may be reflected in it, when two of the satellites may be seen with the naked eye. So says a correspondent. We *have* tried it, and *saw* (seen) satellites of Jupiter," etc. In a late issue of an English magazine of note may be found the same erroneous construction, with the verb *To Come.* "General Hawley *had*, by the aid of our Highlanders, *beat* down two little stone walls, and *came* (come) in upon the right flank of their second line."

Saw is not preceded by an auxiliary verb. *Seen* must be preceded by some part either of the auxiliary verb *To Have*, or of the auxiliary verb *To Be;* as, I have seen,—He has seen,—She had seen,—We shall have seen,—It is seen,—It was seen,—We were seen,—They had been seen,—It should have been seen,—etc.

Did is not preceded by an auxiliary verb. *Done* must be preceded by some part either of *To Have*, or of *To Be;* as, I have done,—He has done,—They had done,—They will have done,—It may be done, —It is done,—It shall be done,—It was done, etc.

"I done,"—"I seen,"—"I have saw,"—"I have went,"—should be, "I *did*,"—"I *saw*,"—"I have *seen*,"—"I have *gone*."

I see for *I saw*.

Persons sometimes say, "I *see* him yesterday," instead of, "I *saw* him yesterday." The words of the first example represent an impossible association of ideas. What happened yesterday, and what happens to-day, cannot be thus conjoined. *To see* is present, *yesterday* is past. One might as well say, "I see him to-morrow," instead of saying, "I shall see him to-morrow," as say, "I see him yesterday." The error is precisely the same, although in the one case mention is made of *yesterday*, and in the other, of *to-morrow*.

There are, however, certain cases, where the ideas of frequent repetition, of constant presence, or of eminent existence, are involved, where the expression *I see* can be employed in speaking of what is temporarily past; as, "I *see* him about the city,"—"I *see* by the papers,"—"I *see* by Hume's History, that he *says*," etc.

Of a distinguished author, we always say, "He *writes*,"—"He *says*." Of such a one, we suppose that his works are animate with the spirit which he breathed into them, and that, through them, he still speaks. We may even say of the opinion of an ordinary person, " Mr. —— *says ;*" because the view reported is supposed to be based on a fixed opinion, and always to find utterance in the same expression.

Come for came.

One of the most common mistakes is the use of *come* for *came;* as, "I *come* to town this morning," —"He *come* to my store." *Come* is present, *came* is past. The sentences should be, "I *came* to town this morning,"—"He *came* to my store."

Has began for has begun.

Has began for *has begun* is frequently said; and also *begun* for *began;* as, "He *has began* to study German,"—"He *begun* to get noisy."

Began is the imperfect tense of the verb *To Begin, begun* is its perfect participle. The sentences should be, "He has *begun* to study German,"—"He *began* to get noisy."

Were drank for were drunk.

A very common error is, "The following toasts were *drank*." The sentence should be:— "The following toasts were *drunk*."

Plead for Pleaded.

Plead, mispronounced *pled*, is frequently used for *pleaded;* as, "He *plead* (pled) guilty to the indictment." The sentence should be, "He *pleaded* guilty to the indictment."

To Plead is a regular verb. The present is *plead* (pronounced *pleed*), imperfect tense, *pleaded* (pronounced *pleeded*), perfect participle, *pleaded* (pronounced *pleeded*).

"Had ought to," and "Had n't ought to."

Were it not that the writer is informed, on good authority, that the New Englandisms, *Had ought to* and *Had n't ought to* are making progress among us, he would not include them in his list of popular errors, from which were to be excluded those errors that are confined to one section of the country.

Ought has only one inflection—*oughtest*, which is seldom used, because it requires to be preceded by *thou*, which, at present, is never employed, except in the solemn style of writing.

The idea conveyed by the word *ought* is positive in its nature. We may with propriety say, "He ought *to do* so and so;" or, "He ought *to have done* so and so." The obligation implied is specific: it admits of no qualification. If a man *ought* to do so and so, he *is* under the obligation of doing it; if he *ought* to have done so and so, he *was* under the obligation of doing it. He cannot with propriety say, "I had ought to do it,"—"I had ought to have gone out,"—"I had n't ought to do it,"—"I had n't ought to have gone out," etc.

CHAPTER XI.

MINOR GRAMMATICAL ERRORS.

"I wanted very much to have gone," etc.

THE next popular error to be treated of is not confined to the illiterate, but is often found even in the writings of good authors. It is the use of two verbs in the past time, when only one should be in that time. Lindley Murray says, " Expected *to have found* him, is irreconcilable alike to grammar and to sense. . . . . . Every person would perceive an error in this expression:—' It is long since I commanded him *to have done* it.' Yet 'expected to *have found*,' is no better. It is as clear that the *finding* must be posterior to the expectation, as that the *obedience* must be posterior to the command."*

There are sentences, of course, in which the use of the perfect infinitive is not only proper,

---

* These remarks are taken by Murray from very nearly the exact words of Dr. Campbell, whom, with Dr. Lowth, he cites in support of his position.

but necessary; as in the following one given by Murray :—"It would ever afterwards have been a source of pleasure to have found him wise and virtuous." But there are thousands of cases in which the perfect infinitive is employed, where the present infinitive should have been substituted.

For instance, you will hear persons say, "I *wanted* very much *to have* gone," or, "He *was* very glad *to have* been there." If these sentences are meant to express the idea that one had wished something disagreeable to be over, they are correct; but if they are meant to express the idea that the actions spoken of are agreeable to the persons, they do not express it, but, on the contrary, imply the very reverse. Yet it is the latter idea which they are generally intended to express.

Let us analyze them. "I wanted very much *to have gone*,"—"He was very glad *to have* been there." In the first example, what I wanted was not *to have* gone, but *to go*, because I had *not* gone. In the second example, he was not very glad *to have* been there, but *to be* there, because he *was* there. In such cases, the first verb is sufficient to fix the time as past, and however long past, the associated verb must be *present;* thus, " I *wanted* very much *to go*,"— " He *was* very glad *to be* there."

The expression, " I *feel* very glad *to have been* there," or, " He *is* very glad *to have been* there," conveys ideas very different from those conveyed by the sentences which have been condemned. In these, the time is established with relation to the *present*, and must be *past*. In those, the time is established with relation to the *past*, and must be *present*.

Repetition of *that*.

In a late paper the following sentence occurs: "It does not follow *that*, because there are no national banks of issue at the South, *that* there is necessarily an insufficiency of currency there."

In this sentence, there is an unnecessary repetition of the word *that*. It should read thus :— " It does not follow that, because there are no national banks of issue at the South, there is necessarily an insufficiency of currency there ;" or, " It does not follow, because there are no national banks of issue at the South, that there is necessarily an insufficiency of currency there."

7

Sometimes the word *that* is improperly omitted. In the same paper occurs this expression :— " Such, at least, is the reasoning of the ladies, and we suppose *they* are right." The proper wording is, " we suppose *that* they are right." In conversation, however, omission of the word *that*, if not too frequently indulged in, is not only correct, but preferable. Especially to familiar conversation, which aims less at precision than at ease, many things are permitted that would be intolerable in writing.

The manifest misuse of the word *that*, has no doubt led many persons to omit it where, otherwise, they would have employed it. Admirable practice with respect to its use, as well as with respect to English generally, is to be found in Macaulay's writings, which are models of conciseness and perspicuity in style.

The postscript to the 80th number of the Spectator, headed " The just Remonstrance of affronted THAT," and referring to the word *that*, not as a conjunction, as in the above-cited examples, but as supplying the places of the pronouns *who* and *which*, concludes thus :—" I am not against reforming the corruptions of speech you mention,

and own there are proper seasons for the introduction of other words besides That; but I scorn
as much to supply the place of a Who or a Which
at every turn, as they are unequal always to fill
mine; and I expect good language and civil
treatment, and hope to receive it for the future:
That, That I shall only add is, That I am,

"Yours,   "THAT."

CHAPTER XII.

CONFOUNDING OF *SHALL* AND *WILL*.

It is not within the scope of this work to treat of all the shades of meaning that can be expressed by the combination of the words *shall* and *will* with the pronouns only, and with the pronouns and the verbs. A few examples of the ordinary mistakes in the use of the words when used in the first person must suffice.

Shall, in the first person, predicts. *Will*, in the first person, implies volition, certainty, power to perform.*

---

* That the use of *shall* and *will*, in the first person, as differing from their use in the other persons, is not founded on a purely arbitrary distinction, will be clear to the reader from the following considerations :

The first person singular is always the speaker, but not always the agent. When the first person singular is not only the speaker, but the agent also, he can, in that double capacity, not only predict, but he can promise. He can say either, "I *shall*," or "I *will*." But from the moment when he ceases to be the agent, the power of *willing* departs from

When *shall* is used in the first person, it relates to what the user believes will come to pass, but what he does not *assert* his power to control; as, " I shall be there to-morrow,"—"I shall buy it,"—"I shall find him prompt,"—" I shall soon be thirty years of age."

Will, in the first person, asserts what, although it may prove to be out of the user's power to accomplish, is promised on the presumption that the power exists. One cannot, however, promise the accomplishment of what depends on

him and resides in another person, or in other persons, and he is constrained to say, *thou wilt, he will, ye* or *you will, they will:* except in one case, where he possesses power over another or others, and then he can say, *thou* SHALT, *he* SHALL, *ye* or *you* SHALL, *they* SHALL. To condense: So long as the speaker, either as the agent or as the master of another, possesses power to control, he can say, I *will,* you *shall.* When he is neither the agent, nor the master of another agent, he must say, you *will.*

It only remains to add that, when used with *shall* and *will,* the first person plural *we* is subject to the same rule as that controlling the first person singular *I;* because, although the word *we* involves the idea of the existence and action of at least two free agents, their action is concerted, and by means of the inclusive term *we,* can be expressed even by one of the number.

another free agent, or of what, by its nature, is immutable. Therefore, reverting to the above examples, although one can say, " I *will* be there to-morrow,"—" I *will* buy it," one cannot say, "I *will* find him prompt,"—" I *will* soon be thirty years of age." It should be evident that the ascertaining of another to be what he is thought or hoped to be, is out of any one's power, and also, that controlling periodicity is equally out of any one's power.

Whatever idea concerns one's beliefs, hopes, fears, pains, likes, and dislikes, cannot be expressed in conjunction with the words *I will.* To demonstrate this, let us examine the three following sentences :—1. I think that I will go. 2. I hope that I will be there. 3. I fear that I will drop it.

1. If one *will* go, he intends to go, and his going cannot be doubtful to his own mind, as the word *think* implies. If he is in doubt, as the word *think* implies, he cannot say, I *will* go, which indicates the determination to go. The first sentence, therefore, should be, "I think that I *shall* go."

2. If one *will* be at a place, there is no use of his *hoping* that he shall be there, for he knows that he intends to be there, as he knows what is passing in his own mind.   If he merely *hopes* to be there, which implies doubt, how can he say that he *will* be there?   The second sentence, therefore, should be, "I hope that I *shall* be there."

3. If one *will* drop a thing, how can he *fear* dropping it.   If he *fears* dropping it, how can he say that he *will* drop it?   The third sentence, therefore, should be, " I fear that I *shall* drop it."

The two ideas in each of the sentences, as first given, are incompatible with each other.

If it seems rational that, in the case of what relates to beliefs, hopes, and fears, to which the three preceding examples respectively belong, we cannot properly use the expression *I will*, equally rational must it seem, that in the case of pains, likes, and dislikes, the other three circumstances enumerated, the expression is not applicable. How can one say, "I *will* have a headache,"— "I *will* like the performance,"—"I *will* dislike the city ?"   Of these and such subjects, one may prophetically say, *I shall*, but not *I will*.

Except indirectly, the power to control the result lies not in the speaker.

Shall, is very seldom used for *will*. Scarcely any one would say, in answer to the question, "Will you meet me at twelve o'clock to-morrow?" —"I *shall*." The question calls for a promise by way of answer, not for a prophecy. It is *will*, as has been shown, that is frequently used for *shall*. The writer has in his possession a newspaper article, in which *will* for *shall* is used four times in two consecutive paragraphs, as follows :—" We will possess,"—"We will find," —" We will have,"—" We will have" (No.2) ;— all of the words being used in the sense of pre-diction, not of possessing power to control, and therefore incorrectly used instead of *shall*.

Confounding of *should* and *would*.

Used in the *first person*, as *futures*, in combination with other verbs, *should* and *would* are analogous to *shall* and *will*—*should* corresponding to *shall*, and *would* to *will : should* simply predicting, *would* asserting power to perform.*

* *Should* is often used in a sense which has been described as defining the requirement of *custom*, as contradistinguished from the obligation of *duty*, indicated by the

One should not say, "I knew that I *would* be sea-sick." What is intended to be expressed is a lively presentiment, which had mentally, and perhaps verbally, taken the form of a prediction. The sentence should be, "I knew that I *should* be sea-sick."

"I *would* be pleased to have you dine with me," means that "I should like to be pleased to have you dine with me;" which is as much as to say, "As matters stand, I am *not* pleased to have you dine with me."

All such expressions as "I *would* like to go," —"I *would* prefer to see it,"—"I *would* be delighted,"—are incorrect; all meaning the reverse of what the speaker intends to say. They should be, "I *should* like to go,"—"I *should* prefer to see it,"—"I *should* be delighted."

Just as, in the first person, in the case of *shall* and *will*, *will* is frequently used for *shall*, but not *shall* for *will*; so, in the first person, in the case of *should* and *would*, *would* is frequently used for *should*, but not *should* for *would.*

word *ought*. We say, "I should not lose the opportunity of hearing so great a prima donna." "He should dress better," etc. *Should*, however, is frequently used in the stronger sense, implying *duty*.

CHAPTER XIII.

USE OF THE WRONG VERB.*

Lay for *Lie*.

Lay is frequently used for *lie;* as, "He *laid* down,"—"He was *laying* down."

The confounding of the two verbs *To Lie* and *To Lay* originates in the circumstance that the form *lay* belongs to both verbs. One can *lay* a thing down. The thing can be *laid* down. But it *lies* (not lays) on the table, ground, or wherever it may be placed. One can *lay* himself or herself down. But, in so doing, he or she *lies* (not lays) down. "He *lay* (not laid) down at three o'clock." "She was *lying* (not laying) down." "They had *lain* (not laid) down."

In 'Childe Harold,' Byron says,

"——in some near port or bay,
And dashest him again to earth :—there let him *lay*."

That, however, was done, by poetic license, to get a rhyme for *bay*.

* Vulgarisms and other errors.

Set for Sit.

Set is often used for *sit;* as, "*Set* down for a moment." The sun *sets,* but a human being *sits.* A hen is generally said to *set,* but she does not —she *sits.*

Lit for Lighted.

"The gas is *lit,*" is often said, instead of, "The gas is *lighted.*" The word *lit* may be used as a colloquialism, but it should not be written, unless in representing conversation.

Lit for Lighted or Alighted.

Lit is frequently used for *lighted* or *alighted;* as, "The cat *lit* on its feet." The word is a colloquialism.

Rise for Raise.

Rise is sometimes used for *raise;* as, "Help me to *rise* this chest." The sentence should be, "Help me to *raise* this chest."

Raise for Rise.

Raise is often used for *rise;* as, "How many feet does the tide *raise?*" The sentence should be, "How many feet does the tide *rise?*"

Wrench for Rinse.

"*Wrench* off those dishes," and similar expressions, are constantly heard, not only among servants, but among people who should know better than to use them.   Dr. Elwyn, in his 'Glossary of supposed Americanisms,' citing Brockett and Holloway as his authorities for the derivation of the word *rench*, adds, "The New England pronunciation is hardly so strong, but is *rens;*" which remark agrees with the writer's observation.   Dr. Elwyn and they, be it observed, do not suppose the word to be *wrench*, but *rench*, an old word with the same sound, and signifying to *rinse*.   Whatever may formerly have been the case, the illiterate now say and intend to say *wrench*, for *rinse*.*

Allow for *Say*.

"He *allowed*," is sometimes used for "he *said;*" but it seems to be employed as a more forcible expression than " *he said* "—rather more in the sense of promised, asserted, affirmed; as, "He *allowed* that he would give me a ticket,"— "He *allowed* that he could not be mistaken," —"He *allowed* that he would sooner die than do such a thing." In any one of these senses,

---

*Brockett gives "*rench* to rinse.   Isl. (Icelandic) *hreinsa*, to make clean.   Dan. *rense*, to clean.   Swed. *rensa*, to cleanse."

or in that of *to say*, it is a vulgarism of the deepest dye.

These senses are corruptions of that meaning of the verb *To Allow*, which signifies *to admit, to acknowledge.* We can with propriety say, "He *allowed* (admitted) that the arguments were forcibly presented," "He *allowed* (acknowledged) that he had been in the wrong."

Learn for *Teach.*

Learn is frequently used for *teach;* as, "I will *learn* you how to do it." The verb *To Learn*, with that meaning, was used by Shakespeare and other old writers, and when they wrote, was good English; but, among the educated, it was obsolete even in Dr. Johnson's time, and it has not been revived.

Love for *Like.*

Although the word *love* may be applied to many things less exalted than those capable of inspiring the passion of love, there are limits beyond which it cannot properly be used.

In its least strong sense, it signifies a lively affection for an object. One may, without shame, say that he loves books, that he loves the Fine Arts, that he loves Nature. All of these things concern one's mental being. We say of a miser, that he *loves* money; not because we recognize money as a proper object of love, but because we wish to convey the idea of the intensity of the passion mastering one who hoards.

It is evident, therefore, that one cannot with propriety speak of loving *food*. If persons really mean what they say, when they speak of loving oysters, cake, ice-cream, etc., it is confessing a deplorable circumstance, which they would do better to keep to themselves.

Like is the proper word to use of the best dish that ever came to table. And, well-cooked dishes are *good, excellent, delicious, exquisite,* what you will—anything but *elegant.* " This pie is *elegant,*" may be heard at half the hotels in the country. *Magnificent* beef and *splendid* coffee are not uncommon.

Predicate for Base.

How the word *predicate* ever came to be used in the sense of *to base* as, " He *predicated* his opinion on the conviction," etc., is a mystery. The word affirms of something, that it involves something else. Contentment is *predicated* of virtue—that is, contentment is assumed to be the consequence of living virtuously. General good health may be *predicated* of a sound constitution. The word conveys the idea of the existence of an inseparable adjunct.

Agreeably Disappointed for *Agreeably Surprised.*

Some words, etymologically considered, have a right to a certain meaning, but do not possess that meaning. They have had it and lost it.

There is no reason why one coming to an expected point (*ad punctum*) should not, on finding it more agreeable than anticipated, be *agreeably dis*appointed. But it so happens, that usage makes the verb *To Disappoint* mean, to encounter something *contrary* to our wish or desire, *vexatious;* and, consequently, we cannot be *agreeably* disappointed, although we may be *agreeably surprised.*

Prejudiced for *Prepossessed.*

"Prejudiced in favour," is an expression to which, etymologically, there is no valid objection. *Prejudice* means, primitively, premature judgment. But although premature favourable judg-

ment can be formed, as well as premature unfavourable judgment, to the word *prejudice* is
reserved the expression of the idea of premature
unfavourable judgment.

Tell any man, literate or illiterate, that
another "has a prejudice," or, "is prejudiced"
(without saying favourably or unfavourably),
and what does he understand?—that the feeling in the mind of the one spoken of is adverse to the person or the thing mentioned.
Under the same conditions, tell any man,
literate or illiterate, that another "has a prepossession," or, "is prepossessed," and he will
understand just the reverse of the last concep-
tion—that the sentiment is favourable. And
yet *prepossession* means simply the *pre*-possession
of the mind by a *pre*-judgment.

Of course, as there are two sides to every
question, a prejudice, being adverse to one side,
must necessarily be favourable to the other;
but this action is indirect, and we cannot therefore draw from the circumstance the inference
that prejudice itself may be favourable. Etymologically considered, as has been remarked, it may
be favourable, but usage makes it unfavourable.

Prepossessed, when used alone, is used in a good sense, and *prejudiced*, when used alone, is used in a bad sense.   We also say, "*Prepossessed* in his favour,"—"*Prejudiced* against him."   It therefore sounds like a contradiction in terms, to hear "Prejudiced in his *favour*."   We hear, without violence to our idea of congruity, "prepossessed *against* him."   The reason of this is, that the word *prepossessed* is not employed so exclusively in a good sense, as the word *prejudiced* is in a bad one.

Dickens, in his Preface to 'American Notes for General Circulation,' published in the 'Diamond Edition' of his works, says, "Prejudiced I am not, and never have been, otherwise than in favour of the United States."   He therefore holds, if he wrote what he meant to write, that it is possible to be prejudiced *in favour*.   However, great as is the genius of Dickens, he cannot, after deliberately endorsing "Our Mutual Friend," besides other solecisms in English, be reckoned in the category of very correct writers.

Get *Under Weigh* for *Get Under Way*.

We frequently see printed, "The ship was getting (or got) under *weigh*."

8

To weigh (heave up) the anchor of a vessel, is to perform an operation preliminary to putting her on her course. *To get under way*, is to execute the manœuvre which includes the weighing of the anchor, the setting of the sails, —or, in the case of steamers, the movement of the engine,—the stationing of the helmsman, and, in fact, all the operations incidental to a vessel's movement on her course. *To have got under way*, is to have completed all of these operations, and to have a vessel moving under the guidance of her helm.

Signalize for *Signal.*

It would be hazarding little to say that, twenty years ago, the verb *To Signal* was employed as descriptive of the telegraphing between vessels at sea; and that the verb *To Signalize* is a substitute which has gained favour chiefly since that time.

To signalize should be reserved for the expression of the idea of one's distinguishing one's self by some glorious deed, or for that of an action's enhancing the brilliancy of any attribute or lesser quality possessed by man, as "Horatius

Cocles signalized himself by the exploit of defending, single-handed, the bridge over which Porsenna's army was endeavouring to advance," or, " He, on that occasion, signalized his valour and his skill in arms."

The addition of the syllable *ize* to the verb *To Signal*, is even more objectionable than its addition to the verb *To Jeopard;* because the change in the former, unlike that in the latter, makes the verb in appearance and in pronunciation identical with one of an entirely different signification.

CHAPTER XIV.

USE OF THE WRONG NOUN.*

Balance for *Remainder*.

ALL expressions, in which *balance* is used instead of *remainder*, are incorrect; as, "The *balance* of the morning,"—"The *balance* of the army retreated," etc.

The word *balance* marks the relation between the two sides of the same thing. Etymologically, it relates to scales—*balances*. In correct usage, it is applied to the adjustment of accounts, or to things which from their nature may be likened to accounts; as, "Our accounts *balanced*,"—"There is a *balance* outstanding against him for his rascally behaviour."

Remainder, on the contrary, relates to what is left of a single thing, or set of things, persons, ideas, or whatever, in fact, is susceptible of being reckoned as a part or as particulars of one whole; as, "The *remainder* of the cake,"—

* Vulgarisms.

"The *remainder* of the trinkets,"—"The *remainder* of the guests,"—"The *remainder* of the arguments, speeches, toasts," etc.

Balance, with its legitimate meaning, was and is used in the language of trade, and there acquired the corrupt meaning with which it has entered popular language.

Reference for Recommendation.

Reference is frequently used instead of *recommendation*.

For instance : A servant girl, seeking a situation, *refers* to some one with whom she has lived, as being willing to *recommend* her. In so doing, she gives her *reference*, not her *recommendation*. Yet the person who wishes to employ her, in case that the *recommendation* prove satisfactory, often speaks of " getting her *reference*," the very thing which had been obtained.

Preventative for Preventive.

No mistake is more common than the use of *preventative* for *preventive ;* as, " Quinine is a great *preventative* of Chills and Fever, as well as a remedy for the disease." There is no word, *preventative.* We should say, " Quinine is a great *preventive*," etc.

Notoriety for *Distinction.*

The word *notoriety*, when used in relation to persons, is restricted to a bad sense—the meaning of unenviable distinction. Yet it is sometimes applied to a distinction which the user regards as praiseworthy; as, "He attained great *notoriety* in the best society of London." Within a few days, the writer saw this sentence in print: "It (a play) brought him in what he then wanted, viz., *notoriety.*"

When applied to persons, the word *notorious*, even more than the word *notoriety*, emphatically marks a bad sense; as, "His conduct was *notorious.*"

We can, without dispraising, employ these words, and also the word *notoriously*, in relation to alleged *facts.* Even then, however, they do not convey the idea of commendable prominence in the associated agents, but merely that of wide-spread public belief in occurrence. We can, for example, say:—"I am surprised that you did not hear of the affair, considering its *notoriety*,"—"That intelligence, not meant for the public ear, constantly transpires, is *notorious*,"—"Measures for a successful outbreak had *notoriously* been preconcerted." The nature of the subjects generally characterized by the words proves that, even when not applied to personal publicity, the bad sense of the words predominates.

As applied to facts, the words are either condemnatory or non-committal. As applied to persons, they are always condemnatory.

Wife for *Woman, Girl, Lady.*

"He married his wife lately." A man cannot marry his *wife.* He can marry a girl, he can marry a woman, he can marry a lady; but he cannot marry his wife. The woman is not his wife until he has married her, and as soon as she is his wife he cannot marry her.

"He married a wife from New York." Well, then she with whom he went through the ceremony is liable to prosecution for bigamy, and he is liable to prosecution for—something else, if he knew that she was married.

"He married a Western woman,"—"He married a girl from the East,"—"He married a lady of this city,"—"He married a widow," are all correct expressions, which may be varied still more, and, with appropriate changes for difference of sex, be applied to the expressions commencing with. "She married.'

Most readers probably remember the anecdote told of Sheridan, to the effect that, when counselled by his father " to take a wife," he replied, "Certainly, father, whose wife shall I take?"*

Hall for Entry.

In feudal times, the *hall* was the great room of the castle, the place where its chief and his family eat their meals at the head of the table at which sat their retainers also, each placed according to his rank. The word has several other legitimate applications; as, for example, " The *Hall*," meaning the manor-house of large estates,—"The servants' *hall*," meaning the sitting-room allotted to servants,—" The *Halls*

---

* The English Bible is high but not faultless authority in our language. We there find the expression, "married a wife." There seems to be no reason why, in that place, the original Greek word γυναῖκα should not be translated *woman*. That is the primitive sense of the word, and we have no reason to believe that, in the passage alluded to, it was used in other than its primitive sense.

The context is the only guide to indicate when the word should be translated *woman*, and when it should be translated *wife*.

of Congress,"—"A Musical *Hall*,"—any large room devoted to the purpose of assembly.

In all applications of the word, size and adaptation to an assembly are indispensable to the constituting of a hall.   The calling an *entry* a *hall* is therefore a misapplication of the term.   In this country there are, as a general rule, no halls in dwellings. When, however, a house is so constructed, as is sometimes the case, that there is a large room at the entrance, through which communication with the rest of the house is established, it may properly be styled a *hall*. But to apply the term to the largest *entry*, is more absurd than to call it a *corridor ;* which at least means a *passage-way* in a building, although it does mean a magnificent passage-way, and the building in which it is must be an *edifice*.

The misuse of the word *hall* has come from the petty motive of trying to exalt small things by high-sounding names.   The effect naturally produced is to debase them.

Residence for House.

The use of the phrase "*my residence,*" for the phrase "*my house,*" from whatever motive it may now proceed, originally proceeded from that attributed in the last paragraph; people having been actuated in this case, as well as in the other, by the desire to imply magnificent circumstances.

My residence is a grand name for *my house*. When thus used, as synonymous with *house*, the phrase is incorrectly used. A man may have *many residences*, but can *dwell* only in one house. He may have *many residences* and *dwell nowhere*.

Nearly every person has some one place which, however little he may stay there, he recognizes, and others recognize, as his home. If he is in foreign parts, he, on being asked where he lives, mentions his country; if in his country, he mentions his city or his town; if in his city or town, he mentions his domicile. It is evident, therefore, that residence in a place, whatever duration it may have, does not, so long as it is regarded as temporary, constitute *living* in that place, in the sense with which we speak of one's living in such and such a country, or in such and such a city, or in such and such a house. What is true of the word *residence*, meaning the *act of residing*, is also true of its *derivative*, the word *residence*, meaning *house*—that is, as *residing* does not mean *living permanently*, so neither does *residence* mean *home*.

The difference between *living* or *dwelling*, and *residing*, may be thus exemplified :—" Mr. Jones *lives* in America, but he is *residing* abroad." "Many Southerners used to *live*, during the winter, on their plantations, and, during the summer, used to *reside* at the North,"—" Mr. Brown's *house* is in this city, but, during a portion of the year, he occupies one of his country *residences*,"—" Lord —— has four large estates, and an establishment in London, and he goes so constantly from one *residence* to another, that he may be said to have no *home*."

It will be perceived that these terms are not interchangeable. In a word, when a person *resides* long enough in a house to constitute it a *home*, it ceases to be a *residence*, and becomes his *dwelling, domicile, house, home*.

"My *house*," although it may also signify "my *property*," is synonymous with "my *home*." We generally *live* (not reside) in this or that *house* (not residence). When we can properly use the words *reside* and *residence*, depends upon circumstances, and can in every case be easily ascertained, if considered in the light thrown on the subject by the preceding remarks and examples.*

* The only consideration that should reconcile us to the word *residence*, as synonymous with the words *house* and *home*, is the circumstance that this use of the word may be regarded as presenting a truthful picture of the social aspect of the United States. With no law of primogeniture, and peopled by an energetic democracy, a country where success achieved by one generation of a family cannot be maintained without the personal exertions of their descendants, presents a peculiar phase of civilization, in a nomadic social condition, in which the tenure of none is so secure as rightly to be deemed more than *residence*.

In the prevalent use of the word *residence*, in the formula of funeral notices, there may lie a deeper meaning than we imagine. Certain it is, in view of the fact that, at longest, man's stay on earth is but a brief sojourn, nothing can be more appropriate than one's speaking of a person's being buried from his "late residence."

CHAPTER XV.

USE OF THE WRONG WORD (MISCELLANEOUS).*

Only for *Except* or *Unless.*

INSTEAD of the word expressive of a certain idea, another, expressive of a totally different idea, is sometimes employed.

On a sign-post, near Albany, appears the following notice :—" The cars will not stop at this station, *only* when the bell rings." It is clear that this wording informs the passengers that the cars will stop, not only at times when the bell rings, but also at other times; from which intimation they would be justified in concluding that the cars would *always* stop at the station, whether the bell did or did not ring. The notice should be :—" The cars will not stop at this station, *except* when the bell rings;" or, better still, "*unless* the bell rings." If desired, the word *only* can be retained, merely by omitting the

* Vulgarisms and other errors.

negative; thus, "The cars will stop at this station, *only* when the bell rings.

Contemptible for *Contemptuous*.

A person sometimes says of another, "I have a very *contemptible* opinion of him." Under the circumstances, to laugh in one's sleeve is admissible, the difficulty is to avoid laughing outright.

A man once said to Dr. Parr :—"Sir, I have a contemptible opinion of you." "Sir," replied the Doctor, "that does not surprise me: all your opinions are contemptible."*

Contemptuous relates to the feeling of contempt experienced by the mind; *contemptible*, to the *object* which excites contempt.

Due for *Owing*.

The use of *due* for *owing* is a very common mistake, and is sometimes made by good speakers and writers.

We may say, "It is *due* to such and such a one, to state that he has," etc. This is a legitimate use of the word *due*, which, in the connection, refers to a verbal acknowledgment, the

* The same anecdote is related of Porson.

justness of making which resembles the obligation of a debt. But we should not say, " The success of the scheme was *due* solely to his exertions;" we should say, " The success of the scheme was *owing* (attributable) solely to his exertions."

In for Into.

The expressions " He walked *in* the house," —" He jumped *in* the cellar,"—and all similar expressions, are incorrect, with respect to the use of the word *in* instead of the word *into*.

When one is *outside* of a place, he may be able to get *into* it ; but he cannot do any thing *in* it, until he has got *into* it.

Quite for Considerable or Large.

" He inherited *quite* a fortune,"—"He has *quite* an amount of building materials on hand."

All expressions like the preceding ones, in which the word *quite* is used as if relating to a noun, are incorrect. It must relate to an adjective. We may say, " He inherited *quite* a *large* fortune;" or, " He has *quite* a *large* amount of building materials on hand." In these sentences, *quite* is an adverb, qualifying the adjective *large*. In those, it was incorrectly used, as if qualifying the nouns *fortune* and *amount*.

We can say quite *tall*, quite *short*, quite *brilliant*, quite *insignificant*, etc. ; but not quite an *amount*, quite a *number*, quite a *fortune*, quite a *house*, quite a *man*—the last a very common expression applied to big boys.

Some for *Somewhat.*

Some is often used for *somewhat*, especially in New England ; as, " He is *some* better to-day," —" He reads *some* and writes *some* and walks *some* every day."

Any for *At All.*

Any, in the sense of *at all*, can be used in such phrases as, " He does not feel *any* better (or any worse),"—" He does not ride *any* more," etc. ; but we should not say, " He does not write *any*,"—" He cannot see *any*,"—" At present, he does not walk *any*,"—" She has not learned to dance *any*."

Convenient for *Near.*

The use of *convenient*, as signifying conducive to comfort, is a correct application of the word. As things which add to comfort must necessarily be easily obtainable, accessible, therefore *near*, a misuse of the word *convenient*, as a synonyme for *near*, has obtained currency.

To say, "The provision store is very *convenient*," meaning that it is very convenient to be able to avail one's self of the provision store in general, or of a provision store in particular, is correct; but to say, "The provision store is very *convenient*," or "very *convenient* to the house," meaning that it is *near* the house, is incorrect: although it is true that the nearness of a store is an important element in its convenience. Nearness, or easiness of access, or general attainability, are, in all cases, merely incidental to the idea conveyed by the word *convenient*.

Either, Or—Neither, Nor—Not, Nor.

"It was *neither* for his benefit *or* for that of any one else,"—"It was not done *either* for the one reason *nor* for the other,"—"She is *not* amiable *or* sincere."

All of the preceding sentences are incorrect. *Or* is the correlative of *either;* and *nor*, of *neither* and *not*. The sentences should be:—"It was *neither* for his benefit, *nor* for that of any one else,"—"It was not done *either* for the one reason *or* for the other,"—"She is *not* amiable *nor* sincere."

9

Bad for Badly.

"He feels very *bad*," is sometimes said as descriptive of one's feeling very sick. *To feel bad* is to feel conscious of depravity; to feel *badly* is to feel sick.*

Good for Well.

"He can do it as *good* as any one else can," is sometimes said instead of, "He can do it as *well* as any one else can." A person cannot do a thing *good*. The proper word to use is *well*.

Either for Each.

Either is often improperly used instead of *each*. The following example of this is given by Mr. Seth T. Hurd, in his 'Grammatical Corrector:' "Suppose an engineer were ordered to erect a fort on *either* side of the Hudson river, and he should build one upon its right bank only; would not all agree that he had complied with the order? but not so, had he been directed to

---

* It is frequently stated that the English never use the word *sick* in the sense which with us is attached to it. English literature proves the contrary: although it is true that the English do generally use the word *ill* to express the idea which we express by the word *sick*.

build one on *each* side of the river; for then he must build *two* forts, instead of *one*."

Both Lowth and Harrison give the following examples of the incorrect use of *either:*

"They crucified two others with him, on *either* side one, and Jesus in the midst."*

"On *either* side of the river was there the tree of life."†

Like for *As*.

Like is often improperly used for *as*. One can say—"Just *like me*," as a child answers its playmate's "I went up one pair of stairs." But one should not say—"Just like *I did*." Yet we hear such expressions as, " Like *we used to do*,"—"Like *we did* yesterday." *Like* is followed by an objective case, not by a nominative case and its verb.

Stopping for *Staying*.

We read every day in the newspapers, or hear in conversation, that So-and-so is *stopping* at such and such a hotel.

---

* The Douay Bible has, "They crucified him, and with him two others, one on *each* side, and Jesus in the midst."

† The Douay Bible has. "On *both* sides of the river was the tree of life."

To stop is to bring progress to an abrupt termination. One can say, "I stopped for a moment," indicating a pause of that duration. Strictly speaking, the pause cannot have longer duration: it is convenience that dictates a modification of the meaning of the word. We may therefore say that a person stopped for an hour or two. Manifestly, greater latitude of construction is inadmissible. The attempt to enforce it leads to a palpable violation of the idea which the word represents. A man cannot stop for a week or a day. If he *stops*, he *stays*, until his journey, or his locomotion of whatever sort, is resumed. The proper expression therefore is, that So-and-so is *staying* at such and such a hotel.

Hardly for Hard.

The labourer is worthy of his hire, but he would not wittingly make the appeal that is sometimes made for him—to receive promptly his *hardly*-earned wages.

Hardly-earned is *scarcely* earned—that is *not* earned. *Hard-earned* is the proper phrase.

Occasionally we read even of a man's *dying hardly*. In the account of an execution is to be found the following sentence :—" He died rather *hardly*, owing to the noose slipping after he had dropped," etc. If he died *hardly*, he *hardly* died, and was unmercifully hung. The writer of the description meant that the man died *hard*, which might, or might not, have been the executioner's fault.

Minny for *Minim*, or *Minnow*.

A very small fish is a *minim*, or a *minnow*, not a *minny*. The word in the best usage is *minnow*.

Such for *So*.

Such relates to *quality*; *so* relates to *degree*. One can with propriety say, "I never saw such a *man*, such a *house*, such a *view*;" because, the expressions involve the comparison of *quality*, not that of *degree*; but one cannot with propriety say, "I never saw such a *handsome* man, such a *fine* house, such a *beautiful* view, because the expressions involve the comparison of *degree*, not that of *quality*. One should say, "I never saw *so* handsome a man, *so* fine a house, *so* beautiful a view.

The phrases, *such* a high, *such* a long, *such* a wide, *such* a narrow, and all similar ones, are incorrect, and should be, *so* high, *so* long, etc.

Most for *Almost.*

Most, as an adverb, means *in the greatest degree.* *Almost,* compounded of *all* and *most,* is an adverb, and means, *very nearly.*

It is incorrect to say, "They see each other *most* every day." This implies that they see each other *less* every *night,* instead of stating that they see each other nearly (or almost) every day.

Couple for *Two.*

Any two things of the same kind, joined naturally, artificially, or morally, can be correctly spoken of as a *couple.* The word is not applicable to two of the same kind of things, merely because they are two in number. The Siamese Twins are an unusual couple, but certainly a couple, besides being two. A man and his wife are a couple. A yoke of oxen is a couple. Even such things as two volumes of a work comprised in two volumes may be called a couple.

Ornary for *Ordinary.*

Ornary is a corruption of the word *ordinary.* The writer's hearing it in early life was confined to its application by the low to the low, and to the restricted sense of *lewd.* Later in life, he again met with the word, in one of the States which shall here be nameless, where it is habitually used by a very respectable class of people who apply it not only in the sense of *lewd*, but in that of *ordinary* and *bad*. Thus used, its effect is at times somewhat startling; for a person will speak of another as being very *ornary*, meaning *lewd*, and will address his child reprovingly, with, "Oh, you *ornary* little thing," meaning simply "You *naughty* little thing."

The word in either sense is shocking, and should never pass the lips of any one.

CHAPTER XVI.

SINGLE NEGATIVES AND DOUBLE NEGATIVES.*

" Did not do (or say) nothing."

THE very head and front of the offending in the use of two negatives must not be allowed to escape notice.

In English two negatives make an affirmative. *To do nothing* is to be in a state of inaction, *not* to be in that state is, of course, to be in a state of action. Therefore, to say, "I did *not* do *nothing*,"—"I did *not* say *nothing*,"—is to say, "I did *something*,"—"I said *something*."

There are cases in which it is proper to use two negatives. For if one be unjustly accused of having done nothing, he may with propriety reply, "I did *not* do *nothing*,"—meaning, as shown above, "I did *something*."

There are many sentences in which two negatives are used intentionally and correctly, and aid in forming a more elegant expression than an

* Vulgarisms.

equivalent affirmative proposition would form; as, "Do not think that he does not appreciate your kindness," the equivalent of which sentence is, "Think that he appreciates your kindness." In every case, however, two negatives form an affirmative proposition. The common mistake committed is in attempting to make them indicate a negative proposition.

"He is not improving much, I don't think."

The expression, "I think that he is *not* improving much," means, "I do not think that he is improving much;" but the common expression, "He is *not* improving much, I *don't* think," means "I do *not* think that he is *not* improving," that is to say, "I think that he *is* improving," the reverse of what the speaker intends to say.

"Did not see him but once," etc.

The expressions, "I did *not* see him *but* once," —"I have *not but* one," are incorrect; if the person who uses them intends to say, that he saw the other *no more than* once, or that he has *only* one of a certain kind of thing.*

---

* If the word *but,* in such connections, retained the meaning of *except,* with which it was anciently used in

To say that a person has *but* one, means that he has *only* one. To say that he has *not only* one, means that he has *more* than one. To say that a person saw another person *but* once, means that he saw the person *only once*. To say that he did *not* see the person *only once*, means that he saw the person *more* than once.

The sentences should be, "I saw him but once,"—"I have but one;" or, "I saw him only once,"—"I have only one."

"Had not hardly (or scarcely) a minute to spare."

To say of some one that "he *had hardly* (or scarcely) a minute to spare," means that he had less than a minute at his command; but to say that "he *had not hardly* (or not scarcely) a

---

them, it would be correctly used. In saying, "I have *not but* one," we should be saying, "I have *not* (any) *except* one," just as we now say, "It is *nobody but* me," meaning it is *nobody except* me—not, "It is *nobody only* me." That the word *but* in the above-cited examples is used in the sense of *only*, will be apparent to every one on a moment's reflection; for no one can fail to recollect having frequently heard a person say, "I *have n't but* one," and then, almost in the same breath, subjoin, "I tell you I *have n't only* one."

minute to spare," means that he had *more* than a minute at his command, and just what persons who say, "I had n't hardly (or scarcely) a minute to spare," do *not* mean to say.

"Do not doubt but that," etc.

When one says, "I do not know *but that* I shall go to New York to-morrow," one uses, if not an elegant, a correct elliptical, idiomatic expression, which may be analyzed thus :—"I do not know of any obstacle to my going to New York to-morrow,"—the other course (not going) presents no inducement to make me abstain from going. When, however, one says, "I do not *doubt but that* I shall go to New York to-morrow," one says the very reverse of what was intended, and states, that the only thing doubtful to his mind is the thing which he means to state is *not doubtful.*

The uncertain tenure of life sometimes induces one to reflect that he may not see to-morrow's sun, but that to-morrow's sun will never be seen by any one is a thought that rarely enters the mind. Suppose, then, that we say, " I doubt not that the sun will rise to-morrow." The sentence means, " I firmly believe that the sun will rise to-morrow." But if we say, " I do not doubt *but that* the sun will rise to-morrow," we remark that the sun's rising to-morrow is the sole occurrence of which we doubt. It is plain, therefore, that we cannot, when we wish to speak of the probability of an occurrence, say, "I do not doubt *but that*," etc., but must say, "I do not doubt *that*," etc.

A late public telegram announced that "A careful canvass of the Senate leaves no doubt *but that* the nomination of," etc. What purpose, except to mar the sense, is accomplished here by the use of *but?* The wording should be, "A careful canvass of the Senate leaves no doubt *that* the nomination of," etc. The following item, in which the same mistake occurs, will be recognized as an extract from a late paper :—" There is no doubt *but that* Mr. Gurr is a swimmer of great skill and powers of endurance." . . . . " Those who have actually witnessed the performance can have no reasonable doubt *but that* it is all it professes to be," etc. Again the wording should be :—" There is no doubt *that*," etc.— " no reasonable doubt *that*," etc.

There is a vulgarism in the use of *but what.*
With the view to simplicity, let us recur to the
first example given, modifying it to suit the
present purpose:—" I do not know *but what* I
shall go to New York to-morrow." *What* meaning, in this case, *that which,* and *but* meaning
except, the sentence signifies:—"I do not know
except that which I shall go to New York to-
morrow," which is nonsense.

Were one to say, "I have nothing *but what*
you see," or, "you have brought every thing *but
what* I wanted," one would speak correctly.
These sentences mean, "I have nothing *but* (or
except) *that which* you see,"—"you have
brought every thing *but* (or except) *that which*
I wanted." Are not these sentences quite different from this sentence:—"I do not know *but
what* I shall go to New York to-morrow."

CHAPTER XVII.

OBSOLETE, OBSOLESCENT, AND LOCAL.*

Disremember for *Do not remember.*

THE word *disremember* is obsolete. It is a low vulgarism.

Despisable for *Despicable.*

Despisable is an English word, but it is not now used in the language of the educated. *Despicable* is the word which they use.

Gotten for *Got.*

Gotten is English still, but it is nearly obsolete. Yet some speakers and writers have an unaccountable partiality for it.

Proven for *Proved.*

Proven does not enjoy the wide use and sanction of good speakers and writers that should

---

* Vulgarisms and other errors.

The word *local* is here used as referring to the whole of the United States. Millions of people elsewhere speak English.

entitle it to take precedence of *proved.* It is
used chiefly in Scotland.

Illy for *Ill.*

Illy is often incorrectly used for *ill.* It has
not the authority derived from good usage.

Overly for *Over.*

Overly for *over* is heard in such phrases as,
"I do not think that he is *overly* bright,"—
"She is not *overly* nice,"—"He is not *overly*
particular in such matters."

The word is obsolete, except among the vulgar.

Biddable for *Obedient.*

There is no such word as *biddable.* The word
for which it sometimes does duty is *obedient.*

Unbeknown for *Unknown.*

Unbeknown is obsolete in good usage.

Sett for *Set.*

The connection in which *sett* is generally
found is in advertisements of china, chairs, fur-
niture, or any articles consisting of pieces of the
same kind; as a *sett* of chairs, a *sett* of mirrors,
a *sett* of china, etc. *Set* should in all cases be
spelled *s-e-t.*

CHAPTER XVIII.

TAUTOLOGICAL PHRASES.*

"From hence,"—"from thence,"—"from whence."

In the words *hence, thence, whence,* is included the idea conveyed by the word *from.*

Hence means *from this* place, *thence* means *from that place, whence* means *from which place.*

Probably no other mistake in English has been so frequently made, even by good speakers and writers of the language, as the use of the three words *hence, thence, whence,* preceded by *from;* many, knowing it to be a mistake, falling into it from the sheer force of habit.

"New beginner."

One may, after having failed in an attempt, make a *new beginning*, and analogy may perhaps be strained so far as to permit us to consider such a person, on a renewal of his attempt, a *new beginner*. But it is unreasonable, although not unusual, to apply the phrase to one

---

* Vulgarisms and other errors.

who is beginning for the *first* time. The expression is a pleonasm—a superfluity of words.

" Equally as good as,"—" equally as good."

As good as means *equally good;* therefore, *equally as good as* means *equally, equally good.*

As good also means *equally good,* and *equally as good* therefore means *equally, equally good.*

In the common phrase, "*equally as good as,*" —one can strike out both *as's,* or else strike out *equally.* In the other common phrase, "*equally as good,*"—one can strike out the *as,* or else strike out the *equally.*

A thing is *as good as* another thing, or it is *as good,* or it is *equally good with* another thing, or it is *equally good.* For example: " This is *as good as* that,"—" This is *as good,*"—" This is *equally good with* that,"—" This is *equally good.*"

" In any shape or form."

How can any one suppose that he is adding to the force of his language by saying, " In any *shape* or *form,*" the meaning of the words *shape* and *form* being identical.

" Robert he,"—" Susan she."

Some persons never use a personal proper name without adding to it the pronoun appropriate to

10

the sex of the individual mentioned; as, "Susan *she* was going down the street, and Robert *he* met her a few doors from her house." This is a very inelegant, not to say vulgar mode of expressing one's self.

"This here,"—"that there."

The use of *this here*, and of *that there*, instead of *this* and *that*, is incorrect. Alone, the word *this*, or the word *that*, relates to one of two things, *this* referring to the one near, *that* to the one more remote. In like manner, referring to two sets of things, *these* relates to the one near, and *those* to the one more remote.

"For to go," etc.

The present infinitives *to walk*, *to run*, *to see*, *to go*, and all others, are not preceded by the word *for;* as, *for to walk, for to run, for to see, for to eat*, etc. We should say, "The child tried *to walk*,"—"The horse started *to run*,"—"What do you wish *to see?*"—"What is wholesome is not always what the palate decides to be fit *to eat*.

"Natural talent."

Talent is natural, there should not be the slightest doubt of it, nor that talent cannot be acquired. It is absurd to say, *natural* talent.

Crabb, in his 'English Synonymes,' says :—
"Talents are either natural or acquired, or in
some measure of a mixed nature ; they denote
powers without specifying the source from which
they proceed; a man may have a talent for
music, for drawing, for mimickry, and the like ;
but this talent may be the fruit of practice and
experience, as much as of nature." This is a
strange remark, as coming from an author of
nice discrimination.   Talent is not only in no
degree the fruit of culture, but its absence is the
more painfully manifest in proportion to the
sedulousness of the endeavours at its cultivation
by a person who mistakenly conceives himself to
be its possessor. True, we speak of a person's improving his talents, but we do not mean that the
talents themselves are improved ; we mean merely
that they are turned to good account. Taking one
of Crabb's illustrations: Suppose that a man has
a talent for music, and that, through devotion
to the art, he becomes an adept as a performer.
His talent is not a whit greater or less than when
he commenced to study.   What he has gained
is the reward of his perseverance, his labour, his
conscientiousness, in having tried to turn his

talent to good account, in having tried to render it productive.

Just in this sense is the word used in the Scriptures, in the Parable of the Talents, from which we derive the sense with which the word is currently accepted. There, talents themselves are represented as capable of increase, because they are the principal and interest of money. The increase, owing to the symbol adopted by our Saviour, is necessarily of the same nature as the principal. The deep and beautiful significance that underlies the Parable, however, is that the gifts of God must, in proportion to their value, be turned to good account in His service, and that He will demand a final reckoning. What return will He demand? The inevitable answer proves that this definition of talent is correct. He will demand, not the talents themselves, but the works that they enabled the possessor to perform. The principal, in the spiritual sense of the Parable, is necessarily lost with life, but the interest in good works, although remaining on earth, is to the faithful servant treasures laid up in Heaven.

Talent is far inferior to genius, still it is a gift of a high order, and therefore exceptional; and, with respect to it, and from a worldly point of view, one may be absolutely destitute.

If these reasons, carefully weighed, establish the impropriety of the expression "natural talent," with greater facility must they establish the impropriety of the expression, "natural *gift*." The word *gift* designates what, at the least, is natural, what is sometimes supernatural, as the "gift of tongues" to the disciples. Yet even the phrase "natural gift" is frequently used. Observe, in the contrast afforded by the two following sentences, what force is gained in one of them by the omission of a word:—"Eloquence is a *natural gift*,"—"Eloquence is a *gift*." Can any one doubt which to choose?

CHAPTER XIX.

MISCELLANEOUS WORDS, PHRASES, ETC.*

"Extra nice."

Extra, contracted from *extraordinary,* is, both as a noun and as an adjective, intolerable when not restricted to certain subjects. A man may with propriety say, "I had to pay for *extra* baggage," "There was an *extra* charge for reserved seats," and so on. But if he says, "This house is *extra* nice,"—"I do not consider him (or her) any thing *extra,*" his language smacks of the shop. Now the shop is a very good thing in its way. Most of us came from it, and are likely, either in our own persons, or through some of our descendants, to go back to it. Directly or indirectly, we live by it, or are benefited by it. Far be it from any one to impugn its merits or malign it. But the language of the shop never was and never will be the criterion of elegance. If we can speak of an "*extra nice* girl," why

* Vulgarisms and other errors.

not speak of an "excellent *line* of people," or of
an "*A No. 1* man," and, if some one has lost a
fortune, say, that he or she "has been *marked
down.*"

The younger Dumas said, in reply to an
artillery officer who at an evening party had
begged him to recite one of his own compositions,
"Certainly, if you will bring your park of artillery here, and fire a salvo."

In general society, one's language should be
untechnical. The thoughts and the language of
trade should be reserved for trade. In society,
people meet, or should meet, on a broader plat-
form. There, it is in extremely bad taste to
"talk shop."

"In our midst."

This afflicting vulgarism is so common now,
that one might imagine the phrase to be stereotyped in some printing houses. It is a pet
phrase. The expression is in the extreme incorrect and, from the immoderate use of it,
ridiculous.

Owing to the form in which a similar expression occurs in the Bible, and to a quaintness
in it characteristic of the whole style of the

Sacred Writings, it is there neither incorrect nor inappropriate. "Now whilst they were speaking these things, Jesus stood in the midst of them, and saith to them: Peace be to you; it is I, fear not."—St. Luke xxiv. 36. "Now when it was late that same day, the first of the week, and the doors were shut, where the disciples were gathered together for fear of the Jews, Jesus came and stood in the midst, and said to them: Peace be to you."—St. John xx. 19.

In the first passage quoted, it is to be observed that the expression is "in the midst of *them*." In the second passage quoted, the expression is merely, "in the midst;" but the clause immediately preceding speaks of the disciples as being gathered together, and "in the midst" means, as in the first sentence, in the midst of *them*.

In the midst means *in the middle. In our midst* therefore means in *our* middle. If one should say, "In the midst of us (or of them)," the phrase may be tolerated; though why one should choose an antiquated phraseology to express what can readily be expressed by saying *among us*, or *amongst us*, is a mystery difficult to solve.* _Verily_ is a good word, but in ordinary converse, _truly_ is preferable.

To guard against possible misconstruction, it may be well to add, that there are certain connections in which the use of the phrase _in the midst_, and of the word _amidst_, is neither antiquated nor vulgar; such as, "He fell fighting bravely in the midst of the enemy,"—"It was a hut in the midst of a forest,"—"Amidst great applause the speaker resumed his seat,"—"Amidst the pleasant scenes of childhood."

"To simply state," etc.

The _to_ of the infinitive mood is inseparable from the verb.   Yet the liberty is frequently taken of interposing an adverb between it and the verb. The following are only a few of the examples of this mistake seen in print within a few weeks:— To _boldly_ resist,—To _seriously_ injure,—To _legally_ acknowledge,—To _simply_ state,—To _deeply_ realize,—To _still_ exhibit,—To _rapidly_ recruit,— To _gradually_ change,—To _not only_ ruin:— the last one actually having two adverbs interposed between the particle _to_ and the verb.

---

* The phrase commonly and incorrectly used, expresses the idea of the presence of some one in a community.

"I do not like too much sugar," etc.

Such expressions as, "I do not like *too* much sugar,"—"I do not like to walk *too* far," are supremely ridiculous. One does not like to have, or to do, *too much* of any thing. The proverbs, "Enough is as good as a feast,"—"Too much of a good thing is good for nothing," show that the meaning of the word *too* is well understood. Why then will people use such expressions as those quoted?

"I seemed to think so and so."

It is impossible, except to some metaphysicians, to doubt the existence of *thinking*, or to doubt the existence of what *is thought;* and persons who use the above phrase are not metaphysicians. We think, when awake, always; and that we think, and what we think, can never be doubtful to our own minds. Hence we cannot say, "I *seemed* to think."

"He has a right to do it," etc.

Singular as the fact may appear to some persons, the phrases, "He has a right to do it,"—"He has a right to see to it," and similar ones, are often used by others to signify, that a certain individual *ought* to do or to attend to a certain thing.

Between one's *right* to do a thing, and one's *obligation* to do it, there is a vast difference. One may have the right to do a thing, and not be under the slightest obligation to do it. This is too evident to need demonstration.

"Just as livs."

Livs is a corruption of *lief*, or rather, of the obsolete word *lieve*. "I had as *lief*,"—"I would just as *lief*," are idiomatic expressions, in the first of which, the words *I had* are the corruption of the words *I would*. "I had just as *livs*," is vulgar.

"A most a beautiful," etc.

The expressions, "*A most a* beautiful,"—"*A most a* splendid,"—"*A most an* elegant,"—"*A most an* awful," fix the educational grade of the speaker at the lowest point known to our civilization.

We should not even say, "*A* most beautiful," —"*A* most splendid," etc. Each of a number of objects cannot be *most* beautiful. *Only one* can be most beautiful, and that is necessarily *the* most beautiful. *Most* is, in the latter sentences, used improperly in the sense of *very*.

Omission of the final "*g*" in pronunciation.

Many persons never pronounce " g " in words ending with that letter, but say *havin, takin, leavin, swimmin,* etc., instead of *having, taking, leaving, swimming,* etc.

Indiscriminate omission of the apostrophic "*s.*"

As in speech the adding of the sound of "s" to the end of a word in the singular number conveys to the *ear* the sign of the possessive case, so, in writing or in printing, the adding of the apostrophic "s" to that word conveys to the *eye* the sign of the possessive case.

Nouns in the singular number, ending in *s, ss, ce, x,* sometimes form exceptions to the general rule for indicating the possessive case.

Mr. John Wilson, in his ' Treatise on English Punctuation,' gives the following examples of this class of words:—" *Moses*' rod,"—"for *righteousness*' sake,"—" for *conscience*' sake,"—" the *administratrix*' sale."

He adds these observations: " This mode of punctuation holds good chiefly in proper names having a foreign termination, and in such common nouns as are seldom used in the plural, —an exception to the rule of forming the possessive singular, which is founded on the propriety of modifying the disagreeable nature of the hissing sound.

"Recourse, however, should not be had to the principle laid down in the preceding remark, when its adoption would cause ambiguity, or when the addition of the *s* is not offensive to a refined ear. For instance, the Italic words in the phrases, '*Burns's* Poems,' '*James's* book,' '*Thomas's* cloak,' 'the *fox's* tail,' though they contain the hissing sound, are not particularly unpleasant, and are far more analogical and significant than the abbreviated forms, '*Burns'* Poems,' '*James'* book,' '*Thomas'* cloak,' 'the *fox'* tail.'"

The test as to whether or not, in any given case in the singular number, the duplicate *s* should be used, is applied by the ear; and, as the delicacy of that organ varies in different individuals, practice also will vary; but there is no reason why it should be discordant. To omit the *s* always, as some persons do in *writing* and in *printing*, is a barbarism as gross as the general omission of the duplicate sound would be in *speech*.

The following examples of the proper use of the apostrophe in nouns in the singular number ending in various letters, are taken from Mr. Wilson's book:

"*Adam's* book, not *Adams's:* the book did not belong to Adams.

John Quincy *Adams's* death was no common bereavement.

" Sir Humphrey *Davy's* safety-lamp.—" *Davis's* Straits.

" *Josephus's* 'History of the Jews' is a very interesting work.

"*Andrew's* hat, not *Andrews's.—Andrews's* 'Latin Reader.'

"For *quietness'* sake, the man would not enter into any dispute.

"Col. *Mathews's* delivery.—*Matthew's* Gospel, not *Matthews's.*

" The *witness's* testimony agreed with the facts of the case.

· "Let *Temperance'* smile the cup of gladness cheer. ˙

" We will not shrink from *life's* severest due.

" There is no impropriety in speaking of the *cockatrice's* den.

"A friend should bear a *friend's* infirmities.

"Like the silver crimson shroud, that *Phœbus'* smiling looks doth grace.

" A *man's* manners not unfrequently indicate his morals.

"After two years, Porcius Festus came into *Felix's* room."*

In a noun in the plural number, ending in *s*, the apostrophe (') is placed *after* the *s* (s') *without* the addition of another *s*.   The possessive case of a noun in the plural number ending in *s* can never be formed by adding an *s* preceded by an apostrophe.   For example, we do not and could not say or write, " The witnesses's testimony," but " the witnesses' testimony"—the plural possessive case corresponding to the singular possessive case, "the witness's testimony."

The following examples of the proper use of the apostrophe in nouns ending in *s* in the plural number, are taken from Mr. Wilson's book :

* On signs, the possessive case of the word *cent* is often put instead of the plural number of the word.   On cars, for example, we sometimes read, "Fare, 7 cent's," instead of, "Fare, 7 cents."

"On *eagles'* wings he seemed to soar,—" Our *enemies'* resistance,"—"The *ladies'* gloves and shawls were exceedingly handsome,"—" He must strike the second heat upon the *Muses'* anvil,"— " Thy *mercies'* monument."*

* The indication of the possessive case of nouns *not* ending in *s* in the plural is too variable to receive complete notice in a work of this character. Some of these nouns in the plural, instead of being used in the possessive case, are used as parts of compound words, as *dice-box.*

In the plural nouns *men, women, oxen,* and others terminating in *en,* we form the possessive case regularly, thus:— *men's, women's, oxen's.* In the word *people,*—which is plural when it does not signify *a nation,*—although we form the possessive case *people's,* we not only do not form possessive cases *mice's, geese's,* but we do not use the words in the possessive case otherwise marked. The words *feet* and *teeth* are not used in the possessive case These examples prove how variable is our practice in regard to the formation of the possessive case in nouns not ending in *s* in the plural number. However, the termination of *s* in the plural belongs to most of the nouns in our language, compared with which those terminating otherwise are not only relatively, but absolutely, few in number.

CHAPTER XX.

TASTE.

On the authority of the proverb, "There is no accounting for tastes," many persons presume to say that there can be no standard of taste. Taste, however, is not a thing, here, there, anywhere, and wherever it is, equally good.

The faculty is common to mankind, but the development of it is possible only in civilization, and general excellence in its decisions attainable only by individuals of fine organization, moving in the highest refinement of that civilization.

Only the passions and the form of man are common to human beings. In all else there is divergence. Men are, first of all, stamped with the seal of their kind, then with that of their race, then with that of their civilization, then with that of their society. Despite of individuality, they receive the firm impress of every one of these. We therefore may observe, that all mankind have the same hopes and fears, pleasures

11

and pains; that individuals of each race have the same tendencies; that individuals of each nation have the same views and ambition; that individuals of each class of society have the same feelings and tastes.

Civilization comprises many degrees of progress, from brutish ignorance to the highest culture of which man is susceptible. The taste of the individual corresponds with the general perception of the sphere in which he moves. Each within that sphere acquires from others and evolves from his own mind what constitutes the standard of taste there. This is apparent from the fact that individuals belonging to different classes of society do not coalesce. They cannot enjoy companionship with each other, because they entertain different fundamental beliefs. The maxims which they deduce from these, their habits of thought, their feelings, their tastes relating to all the minutiæ of life, are at variance. Dickens has somewhere said that two counting-house clerks cannot long sit on adjacent stools without establishing with each other a freemasonry of ideas, thoughts, and pleasantry, which is unintelligible to others.

So it is in all society. The assimilative process is unceasing. If like seeks like, not less does association produce like.

Taste, however, is not an arbitrary law imposed on every one by the force of circumstances. This has already been conceded by the admission that every one exercises influence in the formation of the standard of taste within the sphere in which he moves. With individuality, appear differences in taste among those who find the society of each other delightful. Certain differences enhance instead of diminish the pleasure of social intercourse. They furnish subjects for thought and conversation, in the endless comparison of preferences.

They who most study any one of the departments of knowledge in which taste can be exercised,—and it is common to all except to science, —must, with the opportunity of examining the various objects belonging to that department, make progress in the study. It would be in vain for one who has the finest natural perceptions, to hope to excel in taste, unless he has the opportunity to make many comparisons. Reason regulates, but does not create taste. It is in the application of reason to the comparison of various sorts of things of the same kind, that the principle of taste, common to all mankind, is in some who are peculiarly gifted with intellect and sensibility, developed to a point of exquisite delicacy.

The highest taste in the things which belong to social intercourse is attainable by those only who combine in their own persons, intellect, sensibility, and the opportunity to mingle with the best society: that society which is formed of the educated elements in a civilized community. That society which represents every position in life held by the educated, which includes a certain proportion of people who have travelled, and a certain proportion of people who have retired from active life, is the best. Travelling enlarges the views, retirement from business gives leisure for culture, participation in it develops energy and character. The whole mass of a society composed of individuals so circumstanced is leavened by its component elements.

If, then, we have access to such a society, or, if not, have the opportunity of ascertaining the tastes of such a one, we may consider that we possess *prima facie* evidence of their correctness. We are justifiable in trying them by our own reason, to which all our decisions must revert; but we should consider them the standard unless good cause can be shown why they should not be so considered. The probability is that any large number of persons, who, if only by the force of circumstances, must have devoted themselves to the amenities of life, have made progress in the study, beyond those who, being engrossed by more important cares, have had less leisure and opportunity for cultivating them.

Conspicuous, in one sense, in refinement, in which, in another sense, nothing can be conspicuous, is the observance of those things which make no show. In nothing is refinement so surely tested as in habits of body and of mind. The refined are not nice in their persons because they meet the world: cleanliness is a part of their education, and has become second nature. They do not express elevated sentiments because those sentiments are applauded, but because they entertain no others. A more just idea of a family's refinement can be obtained by a glance at their private rooms, than by a leisurely survey of their parlours. At table, they instantly reveal its grade, for elegant habits of eating cannot be simulated, and the vulgar betray their ordinary ones, either by grossness, or by clumsy attempts at delicacy and fastidiousness.

Refinement scorns pretence. It is not given in any thing to display or to meretricious ornament, but is marked by its simplicity and its repose. Even manners and speech are important in its eyes, because chiefly through them is held communion of mind. It does not debase great things by ignoble names, nor seek to dignify little things with noble names, divest any thing of what belongs to it, nor invest any thing with false appearances.

Vulgarity, on the contrary, loves show in every thing. It has its private thoughts, habits, actions, speech, entirely different from their public counterparts. For the public, it puts on its peacock-plumes, and trails them in the dust, opens its lips to pour forth diamonds, and showers toads.

Yet the occupant of no station in life, from the loftiest to the lowliest, is necessarily vulgar.

The dignity of human nature is the birthright of all: its tenure depends on their truth. Each actor on the world's stage has a part to play, which is well or ill sustained, none through life successfully acting any other than that of his own character. The essence of vulgarity is pretence. In its falsity, to whatever degree existing, lies that offensiveness which is so apparent to the world; which is felt, ridiculed, and denounced, even by those who are utterly incapable of determining the nature of the cause in which their sentiments originate.

CHAPTER XXI.

EXAMPLES OF BAD TASTE.*

"You know," and "says I," "says he," "says she."

VERY seldom does it happen that the educated contract the habit of interlarding their discourse with the phrases *you know, says I, says he, says she;* but so common is the habit among the illiterate, and so frequent their introduction of the words, that the sound of their voices in conversation is often mainly composed of the buzz of these accompaniments.†

The phrase *"you know"* is allowable sometimes, the other ones, never. Time past cannot be described with the language belonging to time present. It has previously been explained, that there are exceptions to this rule: but they do not apply to the case now under

---

* Vulgarisms.

† The use of the phrase *"at any rate,"* is also very common. When the habit is confirmed, the three words are pronounced as if they were one—*attenyrate.*

consideration. Even if it were not absolutely wrong to employ the phrases "*says I*," "*says he*," "*says she*," in referring to time which is past, it is supremely ridiculous for one constantly to repeat that he said what he said.

The exceptional case in which the phrase "*you know*" may be used, is where one narrating something, part of which he is aware is known to the hearer, indicates, complimentarily, his knowledge of the fact, by introducing the phrase in an appropriate place. But as a series of pegs on which to hang discourse, *you know, you know, you know*, is intolerable.

Marryatt gives, in 'The Pacha of Many Tales,' a very good illustration of the absurdity and inveteracy of the habit of interspersing a narrative with "*you know*," and "*says I*," "*says he*," "*says she*." A man, in telling a story to the pacha, has been continually interrupted on account of his introducing *you knows*, has been threatened with condign punishment for a repetition of the offence, and has finally been dismissed to be bastinadoed, it would hardly be fair to say for his disobedience—for his inability to obey. The man's companion, witness of the scene, and interrupted in his story also, and cautioned to avoid his trick of introducing the phrase *"says I,"* resumes the broken thread of his narrative, while an executioner stands prepared to cut off his head if he repeats *"says I"* twice. Let us read the scene in Marryatt's own words. Hussan, the story-teller, speaks:

"I shall never be able to go on, your highness; consider one moment how harmless my *says I's* are to the detestable *you knows* of Ali. That's what I always told him; 'Ali,' *says I,* 'if you only knew,' *says I,* 'how annoying you are!' 'Why there,' *says I ——.*" At this moment the blow of the scimitar fell, and the head of Hussan rolled upon the floor; the lips, from the force of habit, still quivering in their convulsions with the motioning which would have produced *says I,* if the channel of sound had not been so effectually interrupted.

"That story's ended!" observed the pacha in a rage. "Of all the nuisances I ever encountered, these two men have beat them all. Allah forbid that I should again meet with a *says I,* or *you know!*"

"Your highness is all wisdom," observed Mustapha; "may such ever be the fate of those who cannot tell their stories without saying what they said."

Emphasizing some of the particles of speech.

No better criterion can be afforded of relative mental perception in different individuals, than their application of emphasis to what is read or spoken by them. Writers on elocution are prone to assert, without due qualification, that the rules for the art are deducible from nature; that emotion and passion always speak with just emphasis. That nature is the source whence those rules should be deduced, is not to be denied; but, unless we at the same time admit that, although the quality of the emotions and passions in all individuals is the same, the quality of their intellect and their training is widely different, we shall form no just rule for elocution. The language of emotion and passion is shaped by the intellect and the training belonging to each individual. The truth of this assertion may very easily be subjected to test, by comparing the reading and speaking of the child and the illiterate, with the reading and speaking of the adult and the educated.

This is not the place to pursue the topic. The intention of what has been said is answered by the bearing which it has on the common and flagrant error of emphasizing some of the particles of speech. Dickens's burlesque on the practice, in the following passage, will afford as good an example as any one that could be selected.

"'I have draw'd upon A man, and fired upon A man for less,' said Chollop, frowning. . . . . We are the intellect and virtue of the airth, the cream Of human natur', and the flower Of moral force.'" *

Step in for *Walk in.*

No one can walk without stepping; so, in itself, there is no objection to the expression "*step in.*" It is, however, one which, with the meaning of an invitation to enter, is never used by refined people. It is a euphemism, which, in that connection, is an affectation of elegance; as if, in using it, one meant to imply that stepping is easier than walking.

* Martin Chuzzlewit.

There are many occasions on which the word *step* is the appropriate one to use. The following examples will indicate the character of these occasions:—" Step on this chair, and you will obtain a better view of the procession,"— " No sooner had he stepped out of the door than he was attacked by three ruffians,"—" Step under this shelter,"—" Step aside, so that I can pass." On examining these, and all similar expressions in which the word *step* is correctly used, we shall find that the space of time occupied by the act is little more than momentary.

Again, where particular attention is to be directed to the *mode* of walking, the word *step* is the proper one to use ; as, " He stepped along briskly,"—"He is so weak that he steps very slowly,"—" In stepping along the tight-rope, she lost her balance and fell,"—" In stepping over the curb-stone, he twisted and sprained his ankle."

In extending an invitation to enter, or in speaking of a person's having gone out, we wish to draw particular attention neither to the time consumed in the act, nor to the mode of its performance. We refer merely to the result. The simplest manner is to say, " *Walk* (not step) up stairs,"—"Will you not *walk* (not step) into the parlour, and wait for a few minutes?"—"So-and-so has just *gone* (not stepped) out for a few minutes,"—"He has *gone* (not stepped) around the corner."

"Pay a call" for "Pay a visit."

A person *makes a call* or *pays a visit*. As a *call* is a short visit, there is no reason why the expression "*pay a call*" is not, in itself, as correct as the expression "*pay a visit*." But the *beau monde*, whose practice is final in determining such matters, say, "*pay a visit*" and "*make a call*."

"Free to say,"—"Free to confess."

Grandiloquent men are particularly fond of using the bywords, "*I am free to say*,"—"*I am free to confess*." If a man can say a thing, let him say it like a man, without telling people that he is *free* to say it.

Tasty and *tastily* for *Tasteful* and *tastefully*.

Although the words *tasty* and *tastily* have been used by some good writers, they have at present a decidedly vulgar twang. Their special application to the words *lady*, *dress*, and *furni-*

ture, affords more than an inkling of the cause. *Tasteful* and *tastefully* are correct words, without even the suspicion of vulgarity attached to them.

Rig for Dress.

In relation to using the verb *To Rig*, instead of the verb *To Dress*, Dr. Elwyn, in his 'Glossary of Supposed Americanisms,' says *To Rig* "is not in general use with any class, but, as a colloquial vulgarism, may be heard sometimes, though only in fun."

This is an error. Many persons, as well as Dr. Elwyn, do suppose that *To Rig* is always used by way of pleasantry; but the fact is that many girls never use any other word to signify making the toilet.

Babe for Baby.

The word *babe*, although perfectly correct, should be reserved for language above that of familiar conversation. We use it properly in speaking of the 'Babes in the Wood,' and we invariably find it in poetry. The household word being *baby*, *babe* sounds pretentious.

Raised for Reared.

Dr. Elwyn says, "Among the great mass of the people of this country, south of Philadelphia, this word (rear) has given way to *raise*. One seldom hears, 'I shall have difficulty in *rearing* that child,' but almost always, *raising;* and, 'where were you *raised*,' instead of *brought up*."

The use of *raise*, in the sense of *bring up*, or *rear*, is certainly no longer confined to the Southern States, as the preceding quotation implies, and both Webster and Worcester assert.

In the phrases, "*to raise corn*,"—"*to raise wheat*,"—"*to raise pigs*,"—"*to raise chickens*," etc., the word *raise* is correctly employed; but in speaking of the support and education of children, "*to bring up*," or "*to rear*," is the preferable expression.

Buried for Lost.

To say, "I buried my youngest child last week," is surely an unrefined way of announcing so sad an event as its death. The fact can be more delicately communicated by a sentence of equivocal meaning. Even if a woman should say, "I lost my husband last year," no one would suppose that she meant to say she had dropped him in the street, or that he had run away. The phrase "*I buried*" is coarse. It is the expression of the material instead of the moral aspect of

the loss sustained.   It recalls, graphically, a horrible incident of death.   Burial, when it is over,
should appear the minor incident.   The one that
the mind should cherish, the one around which
the affections should cling, is the departure of
the spirit, and its life in the other world.

Casket for *Coffin.*

The scenes of death, as well as of life, test
refinement.   The difference in the sentiments
with which they inspire different persons is
marked through the long interval that divides
a decent funeral from an Irish wake.   What
trifling with a serious thing it is to call a
coffin a *casket!*   "Can flattery soothe the dull
cold ear of death?"   The pleasant name of a
coffer for jewels does not reconcile man to death
and burial.   Dread of death, and repugnance to
decay, are instinctive, and cannot be altered.
The fate may be faced nobly, if not boldly, fear-
fully though trustfully, as is fit in the appointed
mystery; but man cannot, without grievous harm
to his moral nature, gloss the truth and give
the lie to his conscience.

Embalming Surgeon for *Embalmer.*

The process of embalming, although it requires
the use of the knife, cannot properly be called
12

surgery, which is operation on the *living* body. It is therefore a misuse of the term *surgeon* to apply it to an embalmer. It is quite common now to see advertisements of "embalming surgeons." "My husband," once said a woman to the writer, is an "*embalming* surgeon."

This mode of speech does not elevate any profession. It is too evident an attempt to confer dignity by a name, and is suggestive of the speaker's consciousness that the object lacks dignity.

The assumption of the title of Professor, by quacks, and by others more respectable than quacks, is now so common that, unless the title is coupled with the name of a person known to have a right to it, or with mention of a professorship, it means any thing, from a professor of astronomy to an artist in whitewashing.

"Not one of that kind."

"*I am not one of that kind*," is a detestable vulgarism. A gentleman, or a lady, instinctively feeling self-description to be indelicate, never, directly or indirectly, except on compulsion, defines any point of his or her character. When he or she does, the language employed, not being stereotyped, proves that the necessity is unusual, the act not habitual.   Either, if constrained to put into words the idea contained in the phrase, "*I am not one of that kind*," would probably say, "I am not capable of such an act:" which expression implies extremity, the repelling of a suspicion or an accusation.

Independent of the deep taint of vulgarity belonging to this expression, acquired by its use in self-application, it is a low vulgarism, even as applied to other persons; thus, " He is not one of that kind."   It has been used so undiscriminatingly,—used as a byword by the uneducated, —that it is associated with them only.

The phrase, "*the worst kind*," is a vulgarism less offensive than the one last noticed, only because it does not relate to character.   It is a pity that every one who uses it could not be punished as was the merchant who wrote for some flour, telling his correspondent that he wanted it "the very worst kind."

Sweat for *Perspiration*.

In certain connections, the word *sweat* is preferable to the word *perspiration*, but those cases are exceptional.   They are where the subject is serious, where the language is figurative, or where the lower animals are concerned.

In speaking of a horse, it would be ridiculous to employ the word *perspiration*, and say, for example, "That horse is in a perspiration." Every one feels this to be true. There is a reason for it. In relation to even the grosser bodily functions and their play in the lower animals we speak with comparative unreserve. We do not, without necessity, allude to the same when appertaining to mankind. We, regarding ourselves as vastly superior to the brute creation, habitually ignore in like attributes any similarity.

We can with propriety speak of administering a *sweat* to a patient. We can speak of a person's being subject to *night sweats*, an accompaniment of some diseases. In matters so grave as illness and disease, the mind rejects, as paltry, any refinement of language not concerning the grosser functions of the body, and chooses the most forcible term at command.

There is nothing offensive in the word *sweat*, in the passage beginning, "In the *sweat* of thy face shalt thou eat bread . . . . " The subject is not only solemn, but the language is figurative, conveying the idea of hard labour.   The figurative application of the word, derived from the original quoted, is constantly made in the expression, "Living by the *sweat* of his brow." Again, in the history of the passion of our Saviour, we find the word used literally; we recognize it as the proper word, the only word that could convey the sense; and we should reject the other with indignation.

We find, then, that except in medical treatment, the word *sweat*, as applied to mankind, is offensive when it has direct personal application on ordinary occasions; as when one says, "I am in a violent sweat,"—"You look as if you were in a sweat,"—"He was in a sweaty condition." It expresses an extreme degree of the condition described by the word perspiration: a condition which is not agreeable to the sufferer, to the witness, or as a picture presented to the mind.

"Introduced to a gentleman."

Many girls say, "I was introduced to a gentleman,"—"I had an introduction to a gentleman."

Courtesy, derived from the chivalrous estimation in which the stronger sex holds the weaker, dictates its conceding to the weaker the privilege of conferring obligation. A gentleman is introduced to a lady, she is not introduced to him.* The fact is that, inasmuch as they are made acquainted with *each other*, the introduction is of each to each. But politeness ignores that circumstance; and a gentleman, being introduced to a lady, she graciously accepts him as an acquaintance.

There are exceptions. A lady, unless she is an empress or a queen, is presented to an emperor, a king, or any other potentate, or any high dignitary. It would be disrespectful to introduce a distinguished man to any ordinary lady, or to introduce an elderly man to a young lady. In these cases, the ceremony is reversed, the lady being introduced to the gentleman.

It is impossible to arrive at a just conclusion regarding the correct application of the word

* Although the words *present* and *presentation*, as well as the words *introduce* and *introduction*, are often employed in speaking of the ceremony under consideration, *present* and *presentation* should be reserved for the most ceremonious kinds of introduction; in which persons are presented to others of rank, as at court. Persons are also properly said to be *presented* to untitled men and women of distinction

introduction, unless we possess a correct idea of the significance of the ceremony. Is introduction merely a ceremony which makes persons acquainted with each other's names, and constrains them thenceforward to observe certain forms to each other when they meet? To make introduction complete, something more is necessary—the affirmation of the fitness of the introduced for each other's society; and this the introducer, if not the mere agent by mutual desire of the introduced, should tacitly guarantee.

Introduction, save presentation at Court, which is only remotely like the private ceremony, takes place for two purposes. Persons may be introduced for the purpose of transacting business with each other, or for social intercourse, temporary or permanent. The unsolicited introducer takes upon himself a responsibility which, according to circumstances, is either justifiable or unjustifiable. For either of the purposes for which his introduction is made, it is endorsement. He tacitly says, either "This person is desirable for you to treat with on business," or else, "This person is a desirable acquaintance for you in society." Yet how often is not this propriety ignored! Casual acquaintances introduce to each other their casual acquaintances. If a person stops to say half a dozen words to one in company with another, the form of introduction is often employed before escape is possible. Through male and female acquaintances, of whom they know little or nothing, girls are often brought in contact with other persons equally or more objectionable; the security in the introduction diminishing in inverse ratio to the numbers composing the widening circle of acquaintance. Many persons can bear witness that, from this freedom of manners, unpleasant and sometimes disastrous consequences flow.

The rule for the unsolicited introducer to observe is very simple: In business, not to introduce any one with whom he himself would not negotiate; and, as a general rule in society, not to introduce persons who are not likely to see each other again, to meet often, or who, if they are personally unacquainted with each other, may rationally be presumed not to wish to be made acquainted. Unless the formula of the introducer discriminates, and affords these guarantees, his action should be resented, as wanting in the essence of the thing typified: not resented at the time and place,—that would be in worse taste than his,—but simply by avoidance of an embarrassing acquaintance.

'John Phœnix' hits well the prevalence of street introductions everywhere, when he says, speaking of San Francisco:—"You meet Brown on Montgomery street: 'Good morning, Brown;' 'How are you, Smith?' 'Let me introduce you to Mr. Jones'—and you forthwith shake hands with a seedy individual, who has been boring Brown for the previous hour, for a small loan probably —an individual you never saw before, never had the slightest desire to see, and never wish to see again. . . . .

"Each gentleman to whom you have been introduced, wherever you may meet thereafter, in billiard-room, tenpin-alley, hot-house, or church, introduces you to somebody else, and so the list increases in geometrical progression. . . . . In this manner you form a crowd of acquaintances, of the majority of whom you recollect neither names nor faces, but being continually assailed by bows and smiles on all sides, from unknown gentlemen, you are forced, to avoid the appearance of rudeness, to go bowing and smirking down the street, like a distinguished character in a public procession, or one of those graven images at Tobin and Duncan's, which are eternally wagging their heads with no definite object in view. . . . . "

In good society, there are occasions, both in-door and out-door, on which persons, in every respect qualified to know each other, meet and converse without the ceremony of introduction; and to know when, and when not, to introduce persons to each other, is one of the signs of good-breeding.

CHAPTER XXII.

CONCLUDING REMARKS.

THE desire to possess the mastery of one's mother-tongue may be stimulated by a higher motive than that which prompts to the acquisition of an accomplishment, or even to the attainment of what we call information. Far more intimately than most of us are aware, language is interwoven with our inner life. Our knowledge of it has grown with our growth; our ideas have been shaped and fixed by its symbols; our affections are entwined with its endearing terms. It has ministered to our ennoblement, or assisted in our degradation. It both bears and returns the impress of the individual and the public mind. If men wish to debase objects, to disguise unpleasant facts, to appease their consciences, they compass all these ends by words. Great is the relief in words ministering to failings and sins —most lenient father-confessors! Through language also comes to men every elevated sentiment that they possess, their experience of the past, their hope for the future. They cannot afford to dispense with seeing clearly through the medium through which they view all that it is possible for them to learn, and communicate all that it is possible for them to impart; and just in proportion to the clearness of that medium to their mental vision is their ability to discover and to reveal truth.

In the course of time it comes to pass that virtues, vices, even follies set their seal on language; that in proportion to the truthfulness with which it has been used, certain words have retained their significance, or with it impaired, and sometimes lost, present under transparent disguises men's secret springs of action.* When the present era belongs to the past, and the educated of future generations look back on our civilization as transmitted through our language and literature, how mingled with its progress and attainment in every department of knowledge will vulgarity be exhibited in the degrada-

* For an interesting elucidation of this subject, the reader is referred to Dean Trench's work 'On the Study of Words.'

tion of many words by which the attempt has been made to substitute the shadow for the substance of things. To penetrate no more deeply into the subject, let us see how even folly may for some write its history, and for others inculcate its lesson, by a change in words. For the purpose of illustration, we need not seek for an example beyond the pale of our own civilization.

Chief among these words, as offering evidence of the degradation of words by usage, and of the degrading reaction of that usage, are the terms gentleman and lady. What a longing for and an unworthy assumption of a mantle which cannot be snatched, but which falls unsought on the shoulders of those worthy to grace it, are shown by their loss of significance! What pernicious effect their reaction has had on many, inappreciative of their import, blinding them to the dignity of labour, sire of Independence, "lord of the lion-heart," causing them to imagine that with it refinement is incompatible, and associating it in their minds with degradation! How little must the import of the words be appreciated by thousands of both sexes, by whom gentility is thought to centre in money, and by other thousands of both sexes, by whom it is thought to centre in dress!

The sign is ominous when votaries of gentility are ashamed of the names of men and women. How ignorant must they be not to know that all human worth is based on true manhood and true womanhood! How little must they reason not to perceive that, if so, all their existence is the veriest sham! But if they cannot perceive this, how can they be expected to see, that, although manhood and womanhood constitute all respectability, of themselves they do not create the higher rank of which they are the indispensable basis? that it is derived from nature and education, so subtly blended, that whether it was born, or whether it grew, is impossible to discover in the effect.

There never was and there never can be a nation composed wholly of ladies and gentlemen. The sooner the fact is realized and tacitly acknowledged, the sooner will the titles be raised from the mire in which they have been trampled by a multitude of pretenders; the sooner will they cease to mislead and degrade the ignorant, who, unable to discriminate between the essence of a thing and its usual accompaniments, sink in the mire, in the vain attempt to sustain too weighty a dignity.

Of one thing we may rest assured. If the character of gentleman or lady cannot be extracted from every nature, is not latent in every breast, and we may safely affirm that it is not, naught but education can bring it to light in whomsoever it does lie concealed. And education does not signify mere book-knowledge: that is the least of its constituents, and may more properly be termed a concomitant. In proportion to opportunity enjoyed,—careful observation, association, and study are in the path that, under Providence, terminates in the vista of a well-spent life, whence to the traveller lingering on the confines of two worlds, the retrospect may well afford contentment, and the prospect, hope.

THE END.

A LIST OF SOME OF THE MOST VULGAR PRONUNCIATIONS.*

Word.	False Pronunciation.	True Pronunciation.
Again,	Ag-gane',	Ag-gen'.
Apparent,	Ap-pah'rent, Ap-pere'rent,	Ap-pare'rent.
Asparagus,	As-pah'ro-gras, Spah'ro-gras, Gras,	As-pah'ra-gus.
Arab,	A'rab,	Ah'rab.
Boil, (small abscess)	Bile,	Boyl.
Boil, (to boil)	Bile,	Boyl.

* No orthoëpic notation is complete without indicating both the primary and the secondary accent of words, and without appropriating certain arbitrary signs to letters, of which, when so marked, the exact sound, the distinctness, indistinctness, or silence, is indicated by their reference to well-known words. The author has attempted to give, by indicating the primary accent only, by the insertion of the hyphen, and by the use of the generally discarded phonetic spelling, a tolerably correct pronunciation of each word in this vocabulary. As this book is not intended for foreigners, and the words in the vocabulary are in common use wherever English is spoken, he believes the plan which he has pursued to be the best for the occasion. A regular system of notation would not here be read and applied, and if he used it, his precision would defeat its own object. Imperfectly as, from the imperfection of the mode adopted, the pronunciation may here be construed, the resulting sounds cannot approach the low pronunciation of the words, which, although marked by the same imperfect notation, are recognizable in all their hideousness.

13

Bologna,	Bel-lo'ne,	Bo-lo'nah.
Carriage,	Keh'ridge,	Cah'ridge.
Catch,	Ketch,	Katch.
Chair,	Cheer,	Chare.
China,	Chay'ne,	Chi'nah.
Cincinnati,	Sin-sin-nat'ah,	Sin-sin-nat'e.
Column,	Kol'yoom,	Kol'lum.
Contrary,	Kon-tray're,	Kont'rah-re.
Courier,	Kur're-er,	Koo're-er.
Cover,	Kiv'er,	Kuv'er.
Cupola,	Cupe'o-lo,	Cupe'o-lah.
Dagguerreotype,	Dag-geh're-o-tipe,	Daggeh'ro-tipe.
Dandruff,	Dan'der,	Dan'druf.
Deaf,	Deef,	Def.
Decrepit,	Dee-crep'id,	Dee-crep'it.
Disappointed,	Dis-ap-pine'ted,	Dis-ap-point'ed.
Drowned,	Drown'ded,	Drownd.
Duty,	Doo'ty, Ju'ty,	Du'te.*
Engine,	Enj'ine,	Enj'in.
Extempore,	Ex-tem'pore,	Ex-tem'po-re.
Favourite,	Fave'o-rite,	Fave'o-rit.
February,	Feb'u-erry, Feb'u-werry, Feb'oo-erry,	Feb'ru-erry.
Figure,	Fig'ger,	Fig'yur.
Finale,	Fine-ale',	Fine-al'le.
Forward,	Fow'ward,	For'ward.
Fragile,	Fraj'-ile,	Fraj'il.
Girard,	Jir-rad',	Jir-rard'.

* For the pronunciation of words like those marked with a star, see the remarks at the end of the list.

Grievous,	Greev'yus,	Gree'vus.
Gum Arabic,	Gum Ah-ray'bic,	Gum Ah'rab-ic.
Guardian,	Gar-deen',	Gard'e-an.
Hoist,	Hyst,	Hoyst.
Height,	Hite-th,	Hite.
Idea,	Ide'yah,	I-de'ah.
Individual,	In-div-vid'oo-al,	In-div-vid'u-al.*
Italian,	I-tal'yan,	It-tal'yan.
Kettle,	Kittle,	Kettle.
Keg,	Kag,	Keg.
Kept,	Kep,	Kept.
Lilac,	Lay'lok,	Li'lak.
Lineaments,	Lin'ne-ments,	Lin'ne-a-ments.
Mantua,	Man'cher,	Man'chu-ah.
Mercantile,	{ Mer'can-tle, { Mer'can-teel,	Mer'can-til. Mer'can-tile.
Memoir,	Mem'more,	Mem'wahr.
Militia,	Mil-lish'e,	Mil-lish'ah.
Mischievous,	{ Mis-che'vus, { Mis-che've-us,	} Mis'chiv-us.
Missouri,	Mis-soor'ah,	Mis-soo're.
Mosquitoes,	Mus-keet'ers,	Mus-keet'oze.
Muskmelon,	{ Mus'mel-un, { Mush'mel-un,	} Musk'mel-un.
Mussulmans,	Mus'sul-men,	Mus'sul-mans.
Mustache,	Mus'tatch,	Mus-tash'.
New Orleans,	New Or-leens',	New Orl'yans.
News,	Nooz,	Nuze.
Opponent,	Op'o-nent,	Op-pone'ent.

Pattern,	Pat'ron,	Pat'ern.
Pantomime,	Pant'o-mine,	Pant'o-mime.
Philadelphia,	Fil-lah-del'fe,	Fil-lah-del'fe-ah.
Piazza,	Pi-az'za,	Pee-az'zah.
Poem,	{ Poy'em, Pome, Porm,	} Po'em
Poet,	{ Poy'et, Pote, Port,	} Po'et.
Poetry,	{ Poy'tre, Po'tre, Por'tre,	} Po'et-re.
Potatoes,	Po-tay'ters,	Po-tay'toze.
Prairie,	Per-rare'rah,	Pray're.
Presumptuous,	Pre-zump'chus,	Pre-zump'tu-us.
Quoits,	Quates,	Quoyts.
Radish,	Red'ish,	Rad'ish.
Real,	Reel,	Ree'al.
Really,	Ree'ly,	Ree'al-ly.
Rosin,	Roz'om,	Roz'in.
Sausage,	Sos'-ege,	Saw'sege.
Shampoo,	Sham-poon',	Sham-poo'.
Stamp, (verb)	Stomp,	Stamp.
Sword,	Sword,	Sord.
Swollen,	Swul'n,	Swole'n.
Tassol,	Tos'l,	Tas'l.
Terrible,	Tur'rib-bl,	Ter'rib-bl.
Theatre,	Thee-a'ter,	Thee'et-er.

(*Th* pronounced as in Theodore.)

Traverse,	Tra-verse'.	Trav'erse.
Tremendous,	Tre-men'jus,	Tre-men'dus.
Tomatoes,	{ To-mats', To-mat'esses, }	To-mat'oze.
Tour,	Tower,	Toor.
Tuesday,	{ Tooz'day, Tchuze'day, }	Tuze'day.*
Tussle,	Tos'l,	Tus'l.
Tribune,	Tribe'une,	Trib'une.
Turpentine,	Tur'pen-time,	Tur'pen-tine.
Umbrella,	{ Um-ber-rel', Um-ber-rel'ah, New England. Um'bril, Am'bril, }	Um-brel'ah.
Watermelon,	War'ter-mil-yun,	War'ter-mel-un.
Yacht,	Yat,	Yot.

"When the long *u* is preceded, in the same syllable, by any one of the consonants *d*, *t*, *l*, *n*, *s*, and *th*, it is peculiarly difficult to introduce the sound of *y;* and hence negligent speakers omit it entirely, pronouncing *duty*, dooty; *tune*, toon; *lute*, loot; *nuisance*, noosance; *suit*, soot; *thurible*, thooribie, etc. The reason is, that in forming these consonants the organs are in a position to pass with perfect ease to the sound of *oo*, while it is very difficult in doing so to touch the intermediate *y;* hence the *y* in such cases is very apt to be dropped. On this point Smart remarks, 'To say *tube* (tyoob), *lucid* (lyoocid), with the *u* as perfect [i. e., with a distinct sound of *y* prefixed to *oo*] as in *cube, cubic, mute,* etc.,

is either northern or laboriously pedantic,'—a description which applies to the vulgar in our Eastern
States, and to those who are over-nice at the South.
The practice of good society is to let the *y* sink into
a *very brief* sound of long *e* or of short *i*, both of
which have a very close organic relationship to con-
sonant *y*.   Special care must be taken not only to
make this sound as brief as possible, but to pronounce
it in the same syllable with the *oo*.   We thus avoid
the two extremes, of overdoing, on the one hand, by
making too much of the *y*, and, on the other hand,
of sounding only the *oo* after the manner of careless
speakers."—Principles of Pronunciation, Webster's
Dictionary.

INDEX.

www.ingramcontent.com/pod-product-compliance
Lightning Source LLC
Chambersburg PA
CBHW030539040726
47497CB00008B/2519